THE
GHOST
OF
LIZARD
LIGHT

YEARLING BOOKS are designed especially to entertain and enlighten young people. Patricia Reilly Giff, consultant to this series, received her bachelor's degree from Marymount College and a master's degree in history from St. John's University. She holds a Professional Diploma in Reading and a Doctorate of Humane Letters from Hofstra University. She was a teacher and reading consultant for many years, and is the author of numerous books for young readers.

⚓

THE
GHOST
OF
LIZARD
LIGHT

BY
ELVIRA WOODRUFF

ILLUSTRATED BY
ELAINE CLAYTON

A YEARLING BOOK

35 Years of Exceptional Reading

Yearling Books
Established 1966

Published by
Dell Yearling
an imprint of
Random House Children's Books
a division of Random House, Inc.
1540 Broadway
New York, New York 10036

Visit us on the Web! www.randomhouse.com/kids

**Educators and librarians, for a variety of teaching tools, visit us at
www.randomhouse.com/teachers**

ISBN: 0-440-41655-8
Reprinted by arrangement with Alfred A. Knopf, Inc.
Printed in the United States of America
September 2001
10   9   8   7   6   5
CWO

⚓

For my nephew Jack Carlton,
a boy who was truly made for adventure.

With special thanks to the students at
Bridgewater Raritan Middle School for
their many encouraging letters.
—E.W.

⚓

THE
GHOST
OF
LIZARD
LIGHT

PROLOGUE

The ghost's first visit was well after midnight on a moonless night in May. Ten-year-old Jack Carlton was asleep under his quilt, curved against his pillow like a snail inside its shell. His bedroom, an inky sea of darkness, was quiet except for a slight rustling coming from the terrarium in the corner. There, Jack's pet lizard, Ned, was settling in for the night. A wisp of breeze from an open window brushed over Jack's face, lulling him deeper into sleep.

Silently, a tiny paper-thin lid lifted, as Ned cracked open one eye. He tilted his little lizard head quizzically, rolling a green eye toward a narrow beam of light beside Jack's bed. It was a beam of light that Ned had never seen before.

The light was coming from the tower of a small ceramic lighthouse that sat on Jack's nightstand. The lighthouse was in fact an old broken lamp that Jack had bought at a garage sale that afternoon. The lightbulb in the tower had burned out long ago and the lamp's worn cord had been cut, but Jack had been happy to get the lighthouse for only two dollars all the same.

In his lizard mind, Ned searched for an explanation for this new light, but none would come. One thing was certain, though: the light was getting brighter. And as it did, the breeze from the window suddenly whipped itself into a gust that flattened the curtains back and filled the air with the smell of a salty brine. Ned twitched in his terrarium. Salty brine was not a common smell in Ames, Iowa.

Then, without warning, the light began to scatter. And suddenly, thousands of shimmering filaments swirled and spun into the air. Ned stood perfectly, lizardly still as he watched a form slowly take shape before him. It was a gauzy, hazy figure at first, but soon grew solid and more defined.

It's a boy, Ned thought, blinking at the figure that had materialized out of the light beam. But not like a Jack boy, he decided. No, this boy was different somehow.

Ned was right on both counts, for the slight figure standing in the glow of the little lighthouse was certainly that of a boy. He was wearing a short-sleeved white shirt, a cloth cap, and navy blue pants rolled up to his knees. Tied around his waist was a rough belt of rope. His bare feet were covered in sand. He had ruddy red cheeks and a head of straw-colored hair. He even had a twinkle of mischief in his clear blue eyes, a twinkle Ned instantly recognized as boy mischief. But something was different about this child. Something was missing.

Ned jerked his head back, his tail curling beneath him,

for suddenly he knew what was different. He knew what was wrong! All of his age-old lizard instincts were warning him that while the boy asleep under the quilt was alive, the other boy standing at the foot of the bed was not!

Behind the cloudy glass of the terrarium, two green eyes glowed hot with fear. Helpless in his terror, the little lizard watched as the young ghost smiled and took a step toward the sleeping Jack Carlton.

CHAPTER ONE

When Jack woke up on Saturday morning, he had a queasy feeling in the pit of his stomach. It was the way he felt whenever he awoke from a nightmare. Had he had a bad dream? Jack couldn't recall, but he was unable to shake the feeling that something was wrong.

Jack ran his hand through his thick brown hair and looked around the room. His face brightened at the familiar sight of the terrarium on a shelf beside his desk.

"Hey, Ned," he called from his bed. "How are you doing? Are you feeling okay, boy?"

Jack climbed out of bed, went over to the terrarium, and tried to coax Ned onto his finger. But the little lizard stood still as a stone and wouldn't budge from behind his tree branch. Jack had never known his lizard to be so withdrawn.

"I don't blame you," Jack sighed. "You're probably tired of being cooped up all day while I'm at school. Is that it? Are you bored?"

Ned stuck his head out from behind the branch and gave his owner a wary look. He wanted to tell Jack that he was certainly not bored, not after last night. He wanted to tell Jack all about the ghost he had seen, how it had walked right up to Jack's bed and stood there, smiling.

But Ned was a lizard and, being a lizard, could only blink his eyes and flick his tongue. He figured that Jack would just have to find out about the ghost on his own.

"I know it's hard staying in here all day," Jack whispered. "And I'd take you outside if I didn't have all of these math problems to do. You see, my dad thinks extra schoolwork will make me smarter, but it only makes me bored."

Ned gazed out at Jack from his terrarium, then blinked. He was a lizard of great sympathy. Jack had seen that the first time he met Ned at the pet shop.

He gently lifted the little lizard out of the terrarium, and together the two headed across the room and assumed their favorite position for long conversations. Jack stretched out on his bed, with his hands behind his head, while Ned settled on Jack's stomach, his tail curled over Jack's belly button. Ned was an astute listener in his calm, lizard way, and he never interrupted. The two spent many a happy hour together.

They had just gotten comfortable when Jack heard the sound of harmonica music floating up the stairs and into the hall. He smiled. His best friend, Denton, was on his way up. Denton had gotten a harmonica for his birthday, and since then he never went anywhere without it. The sound of a familiar melody grew louder.

Denton strolled into the room. His unbrushed red hair

stood straight up on his head, and his freckled nose wrinkled with each new note he blew. As usual, he was playing "Happy Birthday." It was the only song Denton ever played. In fact, every time he tried to play a new melody it ended up sounding like "Happy Birthday."

"Maybe if you got a music book you could learn a new song," Jack suggested as he placed Ned back in the terrarium.

"Maybe, but this one works for today," Denton sighed, and tucked his harmonica into the back pocket of his jeans.

"How come?" Jack asked.

"Because today is Runt's birthday," Denton said softly. "At least the day he and I celebrated it. Wherever he is, I just hope he's getting some cake."

Jack nodded sadly. Denton's lizard, Runt, had walked away (actually, scurried away was more like it) from a lizard outing with Denton and Ned in the park almost three weeks earlier. Even though they had finally given up any hope of finding the runaway Runt, Denton still couldn't bring himself to buy a new lizard.

"Did you know that your T-shirt is on inside out?" Jack asked, trying to change the subject.

Denton McCormic lived with his father in a house across the street from the Carltons. Neither of the McCormics was overly concerned with appearances.

"Huh?" Denton mumbled, looking down at his shirt. "Oh, yeah," he said. "It was only dirty on the outside, so I turned it around."

Denton walked over to the table beside Jack's bed and picked up the little ceramic lighthouse. He poked his finger into the opening at the top.

"Where did you get this?" he asked.

"I got it when I went to a garage sale with my mom yesterday," Jack told him. "I wanted it because of the lighthouse, but the woman who sold it to me told me it's a lamp, too."

"It looks broken to me," Denton said as he pulled on the end of the cut cord.

"That's what I thought at first," Jack agreed. "But maybe it's not that kind of lamp."

"What do you mean?" Denton asked.

Jack took the lighthouse from him and held it up. "Maybe it's like one of those lamps that you rub and a genie comes out," he whispered, running his hand down the side of the tower.

"The only thing that's going to come out of that thing is dust," Denton said matter-of-factly. "Besides, those lamps with genies don't look like lighthouses. But I bet my dad could fix this one so the light works. Why don't you bring it over to my house and let him have a look at it?"

"I can't now, Dent." Jack sighed as he placed the lamp back on the night table. "I've got to do a whole page of math problems before I can go anywhere."

"You've got to be the only kid in America whose father makes him do extra math on Saturday mornings," said Denton, shaking his head.

"You know how my dad is about school," Jack groaned. "He says that if I'm ever going to improve my grades, I've got to exercise my mind, even on the weekends."

"My dad makes me do homework during the week," Denton said, "but he doesn't care if my mind goes all flabby on Saturdays and Sundays. Then again, he's not the principal."

"I'd give anything to have a regular dad who left my brain alone on the weekends," Jack said, tapping the side of the terrarium. Ned was chewing the edge of a lettuce leaf.

"I think your brain gets a pretty good workout all the time," Denton assured him. "You always come up with the best ideas. That takes thinking, doesn't it?"

"Yeah, but my dad doesn't see it that way. He says that every time my imagination works overtime it gets me into trouble."

"You mean like the time you got the idea to have Ned run for student council?" Denton giggled. "That was great! Did you know that Timmy Feeley still thinks Ned Carlton is a student?"

"Those were good posters I made for him," Jack said wistfully. "'Vote for Ned Carlton: He's Lean, Mean, and Green' and 'Reptiles Rule.'"

"Too bad your dad made you take them down before the election, because I know a lot of kids who were planning on voting for him," Denton said.

"Probably would have won by a landslide," Jack sighed. "Instead, I got two weeks with no TV. I probably won't be able to watch TV till I'm a senior citizen at this rate."

Denton shook his head. "I still don't see why you had to get punished."

"My dad said it was because I was setting a bad example and he was afraid other kids would try it. Brendan Farnes *did* say he might run his tarantula for treasurer next year, but who's going to vote for a spider? My dad wouldn't allow it, anyhow."

"That's the problem with having a father who's the principal at your own school," Denton declared.

"He finds out everything I do," Jack moaned.

Denton nodded sympathetically. "There should be a law."

Jack smiled. He could always count on Denton to back him up, just like a brother would. And like brothers, the two had learned how to do all the major things in their lives together, from potty training to lizard training. Denton was his one true friend. Aside from Ned, that is.

"Why don't we work on the lamp later, after I finish my work sheet?" suggested Jack. "Or we could polish your rock collection instead."

"I don't know if I'll be home," Denton said. "I was planning on going over to the cemetery. Wanna come?"

"The cemetery? Who died?" asked Jack.

"Pretty much everybody there," Denton joked.

Jack rolled his eyes. "You know what I mean."

"No one died," Denton told him. "But Tony Panelli bet Danny Ruckman twenty dollars that he wasn't brave enough to lie down on the soldier's tomb."

"You mean the grave with the little flags on it?" asked Jack.

"That's the one," Denton said. "And the rumor is that the soldier's ghost will haunt anyone who lies down on his grave."

"Who would want to lie down on a ghost's grave?"

"Danny Ruckman would for twenty bucks."

"I wouldn't do it for twenty bucks," Jack decided. "But I might do it for a hundred, though I wouldn't want to do it all alone."

"If you agreed to do it, I guess I'd have to go along with you," Denton told him.

"You'd do that for me?" Jack asked.

Denton shot him a sheepish grin. "I can't let you go off and lie down in a cemetery all alone. Besides, maybe the ghost would like hearing 'Happy Birthday.'" Denton pulled out his harmonica and played a riff.

"Do you really think there are ghosts in the graveyard, Dent?"

"Probably," Denton mumbled over his harmonica. "I mean, just think of all the tombstones and creepy statues there."

At that moment, Mrs. Carlton called, "Jaaaaaaack, breakfast!" from the bottom of the stairs. After a pause, she added, "And hurry, your father has an announcement."

"Coming!" Jack yelled as he walked over to the terrarium to check on Ned, who was now curled around his water dish.

"Hey, I have an idea," Denton said, picking up the little ceramic lamp from the night table. "Why don't we put the lighthouse in Ned's terrarium? That way he can pretend he's a sailor."

"Good idea, Dent." Jack smiled. "And if it really is a magic lamp and a genie comes out, Ned can make a wish."

On hearing this, the little lizard raced back behind the tree branch to hide. His green eyes blinked furiously as he watched Jack reach for the lamp and gently place it in a corner of the terrarium.

"Wish for something good, Ned," Jack called over his shoulder as he and Denton left the room.

But Ned's only wish was to get as far away from the strange lamp as he could. For the instant the bedroom door closed, a thin beam of light flickered on and off at the top of the little lighthouse. With his tiny lizard heart beating wildly, Ned fixed his eyes on the glowing tower.

The silence of the room was suddenly broken by a ghostly giggle. This was followed by a low whisper, so low that Ned leaned forward to hear. And the words he heard were so startling that they sent a shiver down his trembling green body, straight through to his tail.

"I don't suppose they'll find any ghosts in the graveyard," the voice declared. "I don't know why people always expect us to be there. Cemeteries are so quiet and awfully boring. No, your Jack won't find me behind any tombstones. I can promise you that," the whispery voice said. "But we will meet again, you and me and Jack. At midnight, at the ocean's edge. Look for me there, lizard. Look for me there…"

CHAPTER TWO

Jack said good-bye to Denton at the front door and then headed for the kitchen. His five-year-old sister, Franny, came running into the hall to meet him.

Franny's curly brown hair stuck out of a bright green bathing cap. She wore blue rubber flippers on her feet, little round swimming goggles over her eyes, and a red plastic stethoscope around her neck. In her hand she held a toy doctor's bag.

"Oh, not again," Jack groaned as Franny tried to put a tiny Band-Aid on his arm.

"Emergency, emergency," she shouted into a plastic toy cell phone. "This is the vet, Doctor Franny. I've got a sick whale here." She turned to Jack. "It's okay, whale. The ambulance is coming. They'll take you to the hospital."

"Whales don't go to hospitals," Jack snapped. "And I am not a whale and you are not a vet."

"No, but I'm going to be one when I grow up," Franny informed him. "And I want to be able to help all kinds of animals, even whales."

Her big dark eyes were full of concern as she tried to look up Jack's nose.

"Did you know that you have some yucky stuff stuck up in your blowhole?" she asked in a serious tone.

"Will you cut it out! Mom, tell her to leave me alone," Jack complained, pulling the Band-Aid off his arm.

"Franny, leave your brother alone," Mrs. Carlton called from the kitchen. "If you have to treat someone, you can come and treat Huxley. I think he's gone into a coma. See if you can bring him back to life."

"Code red, code red," Franny shouted as she retrieved the Band-Aid from Jack's hand. Then she ran back into the kitchen, where Huxley, the family's goldfish, was napping in his bowl on the counter.

Jack walked into the kitchen and found a giant ladybug standing at the stove, flipping pancakes. The ladybug was actually his mother. Mrs. Carlton was a costume designer. She sold her designs to costume companies and was always trying out her prototypes on the family.

"What do you think?" she asked, turning to reveal a set of red-and-black-spotted wings.

Jack grinned. His mother was a short round woman with a big friendly smile. Dressed in her red-and-black-spotted suit, she did make a good ladybug.

"It's better than the lollipop," Jack said, taking a seat at the table.

"Oh, but I'm still perfecting that one," Mrs. Carlton protested.

"Could we please leave the lollipops and ladybugs for a

minute," Mr. Carlton grumbled, pacing back and forth in front of the sink.

"Sorry, hon," Mrs. Carlton murmured.

"What's going on?" Jack asked, noticing his father's wrinkled brow.

Mr. Carlton looked over at his wife, then back at Jack. "I've taken a new job," he announced.

"You're not going to be our principal anymore?" Jack gasped. To be a regular student, not the principal's son, was something he had wished for since the second grade.

"I'm leaving Spring Farm School. I've decided to take a position somewhere else," Mr. Carlton said.

Jack tried to suppress a grin.

"The only hitch," Mr. Carlton continued, his voice becoming edgy, "is that the school is not in Iowa."

"So where is it?" Jack asked.

Mr. Carlton ran his hand over his bald spot and took a deep breath. "It's in Maine," he finally answered. "Your mother and I have been talking about making a big change for some time now, and we've always loved Maine. It'll be a great place for you kids to grow up."

"There will be less stress for your dad, and he can spend more time with us," Mrs. Carlton added.

Mr. Carlton had suffered a heart attack the summer before, and the doctors told him he needed to cut down his stress.

"So it looks as if we'll all be moving at the end of the summer to Minty, Maine," Mrs. Carlton said. "Isn't that exciting?"

Jack sat, dumbfounded, trying to take this in.

"Forever? We're staying there forever, not just for the summer?"

Mr. Carlton nodded. "We're going to make our home there."

"But it's—it's so far away," Jack sputtered.

"It's about fifteen hundred miles away," his father said. "We'll be moving to the far end of the country."

More like the far end of the planet, Jack thought miserably. The far end of nowhere.

He liked visiting Maine well enough for vacation. But he had never imagined living in a place like that year round. He vaguely remembered walking through the sleepy little village of Minty. He remembered that it was a very short walk.

"Do they have a Chuck E. Cheese's there?" Franny asked as she put her stethoscope up to Huxley's bowl. Next to playing vet, eating burgers at Chuck E. Cheese's was Franny's all-time favorite thing to do.

"I don't think so," Mrs. Carlton replied. "But they might have a Louie's Lobsters."

"What about Denton?" Jack asked, his throat suddenly tightening.

Mr. and Mrs. Carlton traded uneasy looks.

"Maybe Denton can come for a visit sometime," Mr. Carlton said. "Don't worry, son, you're bound to make new friends once we get settled in."

Jack couldn't believe what he was hearing. How could they think he'd ever find someone to take Denton's place? How was he ever going to find a friend who could talk for hours about lizards and lie down in cemeteries with him?

"Of course it's going to be a big change for us," Mr. Carlton said, seeing Jack's stricken face. "But I know we can all settle in, once we get used to it. A realtor is looking for a house we can rent for the first semester."

"Oh, honey, it'll be all right. Minty will be a great place to live, you'll see," Mrs. Carlton said as she wrapped her black ladybug arms around Jack in a hug. "And they have some of the foggiest weather in the United States," she added excitedly. "They almost got into the *Guinness Book of World Records* for the most fog in the country!"

Jack frowned. He didn't see how all that fog was supposed to make him feel any better.

"Most of the people in town are fishermen," his father continued. "It's going to be a very different lifestyle, slower, calmer. Why, the entire elementary school has only seventy-seven students in it!"

Jack's shoulders slumped at this news.

"Oh, great," he groaned. "So what you're saying is that we're moving to some tiny town that's full of fog, smells like fish, and has almost no kids in it."

"Just think of it as an adventure," suggested Mrs. Carlton as she placed a plate of pancakes on the table. "We can have picnics on the beach, and we'll be meeting new people and having all kinds of new experiences, living right at the ocean's edge."

Great, Jack thought. And just who am I supposed to meet at the edge of the ocean?

CHAPTER THREE

Jack climbed back up to his bedroom and tried working on his math problems. But he had a hard time concentrating. All he could think about was the move. When he heard the sound of "Happy Birthday" drifting up the stairs again, Jack felt his stomach tighten. He put his head down on his desk.

"What's wrong?" Denton appeared in Jack's doorway. "Haven't you finished your math yet?"

"No, but that's not it." Jack paused, then looked up at Denton. "My dad took a new job, and we're moving to Maine."

"Maine? You mean like in the state of Maine?"

"That's exactly what I mean." Jack sighed.

"But you can't!" Denton cried. "I mean, you've always lived here. We've always lived across the street from each other. What's going to happen to us if you move all the way to Maine?"

"I don't think there are any ifs about it," Jack said. "My parents have already talked to a realtor."

Denton sat down on Jack's bed, and the two boys discussed emergency plans on how they could remain together. They talked about running away, but they didn't know where to go. They talked about Denton moving in with the Carltons or Jack moving in with Denton and his father, but they knew their parents would never agree to it.

Jack spent the following weeks dreaming up schemes that would keep him in Iowa. His favorite one had him sneaking into the McCormics' house and living there, hidden for the rest of his life in Denton's closet. Denton could sneak food and candy in to him. He was the kind of friend who would do that.

But then Jack remembered the stale-tasting mint candies in the glass bowl on Denton's dining room table. And he thought about the nasty tuna fish casseroles Mr. McCormic always made. Jack hated tuna fish casserole.

He wondered what it would be like living in Denton's closet, where there was always a huge pile of dirty clothes. He imagined living his life there, alone in the dark, smelling dirty socks and eating stale mints and tuna fish day after day. He decided to come up with a better plan.

If he had had more time, Jack might have been able to come up with a scheme that kept him in Iowa. But things were happening much too fast. Soon after the realtor put the For Sale sign up in the Carltons' front yard, a couple made a down payment on their house. Things moved even faster after that.

School was out for summer vacation, and the weeks seemed to fly by. And then the dreaded day arrived. They were moving! It was really happening. All along, Jack had been praying that it was some big mistake or a bad dream he would wake up from.

Even up to the final moment, as he and Denton stood out on the driveway, saying their last good-byes, Jack hoped for a miracle that would let him stay.

Denton had brought along a grocery bag full of presents for everyone. He reached in and pulled out a gift-wrapped box of sparkly Band-Aids for Franny to use on her patients. Then he pulled out a head of lettuce wrapped in Christmas paper for Ned. After these had been handed out, he turned to Jack.

"I wanted to give you something special to remember me by," Denton said softly. He reached into the bag and pulled out his harmonica. He pressed it into Jack's hand. Jack felt a lump in his throat as his fingers tightened around the harmonica's smooth surface.

"I won't play anything but 'Happy Birthday' on it," he promised.

"I don't think it will let you play anything else," Denton joked.

Jack gave Denton a small bag of rocks for his rock collection, including an amethyst that Denton had wanted. The two promised to write, and to e-mail when Denton got a computer. Then, feeling embarrassed by the tears in his eyes, Jack hurried into the car.

As his father slowly backed the car down the driveway, Jack leaned out the window to wave good-bye. He wanted to fix his best friend in his mind, so he'd always remember him.

"Hey, Dent," Jack yelled. "Did you know that your T-shirt is on inside out?"

He watched as Denton bent his unruly mop of red hair over his shirt. And when he lifted his head, he was wearing a sheepish grin. It was a look Jack would always remember.

"We're off on our adventure to Maine," Mr. Carlton said cheerily as they drove out of town.

"Off to the far end of nowhere," Jack whispered under his breath. It was the last thing he said for hours. There had been no miracle to let him stay. He was on his way to Maine.

CHAPTER FOUR

Ned seemed as upset about the move as Jack. He paced back and forth in his terrarium on the floor of the back seat. He seemed anxious and jittery. Jack thought he understood. Ned didn't want to move to Maine any more than he did.

"You know, we have a big surprise for you kids," Mrs. Carlton said from the front seat as they crossed the Iowa state line.

"Can we have it now?" Franny asked. She was dressed in a silvery alien costume that she had insisted on wearing for the trip.

"No, you'll have to wait. You'll find it at our new house," their mother explained.

"I thought Dad said it was an old house," Jack interrupted.

Mr. Carlton, behind the steering wheel, nodded. "Yes, that's right, it is an old house. But it's going to be a new and unusual experience living there. I can promise you that."

"And the house sits beside this very big surprise," Mrs. Carlton said.

"Chuck E. Cheese's!" Franny cried. "Will Chuck E. Cheese's be our neighbor? Is that the big surprise?"

"Will you get over Chuck E. Cheese's?" Jack groaned.

"No, honey," Mrs. Carlton said. "I've already told you. They don't have a Chuck E. Cheese's where we're going."

"Why?" Franny asked. "Why don't they have a Chuck E. Cheese's?"

The long drive to Maine was off to a bad start. Franny kept trying to feed Ned, dropping bits of her peanut-butter-and-jelly sandwich into his terrarium.

Ned, being the well-mannered lizard that he was, never complained as chunks of bread and blobs of jelly landed on his head. Jack complained, though, and loudly.

"Stop throwing food on Ned!" he howled. "He's not a garbage can, he's a lizard!"

"He likes peanut butter and jelly," Franny explained.

"Does not!"

"Does too!"

"Does not!"

"Mom!"

The trip out to Maine took forever. Jack tried several times to play the harmonica, but he choked up at the thought of never seeing Denton again and quickly put it away. They had stopped to sleep in a motel in Pennsylvania, and the next day they drove out of one rainstorm in New York and into another in Vermont. Jack felt as if they would never get there.

Franny spent most of her time doctoring her stuffed animals. Two teddy bears died of a mysterious disease in New York State, and a stuffed bunny succumbed in Connecticut. Jack offered to help dispose of the bodies by throwing them out the window, but Franny rejected his offer with a loud "Don't!"

Mrs. Carlton suggested they all sing. They sang along to a few songs on the radio, and when they stopped, Franny continued to hum. She hummed as they crossed the Maine border and was still humming when they reached the sleepy little village of Minty. The constant clicking of the windshield wipers finally ceased as the car slowed down.

"Close your eyes," Mr. Carlton commanded as they neared their new address.

Both Jack and Franny, worn out with arguing for the last two hundred miles of the drive, readily did as they were told. Franny put her hands over her eyes. Jack took a deep breath, hoping that somehow this big surprise could make him feel better.

"Now?" Franny squeaked, peeking over her fingers.

"Now," Mrs. Carlton called back as the car pulled into a graveled drive.

Jack opened his eyes and looked through the lingering fog at the white shingled cottage before them. Then his eyes traveled from the front door, down a long wooden walkway. The walkway led to a tall white tower that seemed to rise out of the flat gray rocks it sat on. From atop the tower, a beam of light shone. Beyond that, as far as he could see, there was nothing but ocean.

"It's a lighthouse!" Jack exclaimed, getting out of the car. "It's almost like my lamp!"

"It's called Lizard Light," Mr. Carlton said, coming up beside him. "From the sea, that piece of land with the lighthouse on it looks like a lizard's tail. That's why they call our lighthouse Lizard Light."

"*Our* lighthouse?" Jack croaked.

"Well, not officially ours," Mr. Carlton admitted. "It really belongs to the state. The Coast Guard maintains the light. And it's locked, so we can't go inside. But we'll be living in the keeper's house. And the tower does go with the house."

"It's so exciting!" Mrs. Carlton was beaming. She reached out and pulled Jack and Franny to her in a hug. "Did you kids ever imagine that we'd be living beside a lighthouse?"

Actually, Jack *had* imagined that once, after reading a book about a lighthouse keeper's daughter. But that had just been another one of his many made-up stories, like living in a jungle or on another planet. It was fun to imagine, but not something that was really supposed to happen!

If only the lighthouse could have been back home in Iowa instead of in Minty, Maine, Jack thought, then he could have enjoyed it. He and Denton could have enjoyed it together. But here, clear across the country, fifteen hundred miles away from his best friend, what good was it?

A light rain was falling, so they all headed inside, Jack with the terrarium in his arms. The house was old, more than a hundred years old, according to the realtor. At the entrance, spelled out in flat pebbles over the arched doorway, were the words *Neversink Cottage*. Jack had never lived in a house that had its own name.

"Must have been the keeper's credo," suggested Mr. Carlton.

Once inside, Jack sensed immediately how different this house was from their home in Iowa. Their house in Ames had been brand-new, and so was everything around it. But this old house seemed to be all about somebody else.

Neversink Cottage had a whispery feel to its low-beamed ceilings, and the bubbly glass in the windows held the memories of fingers pressed against it long ago. The wide window seats were worn smooth from someone else's waiting and watching.

Jack was not the only one to notice the difference. Mr. and Mrs. Carlton lowered their voices to hushed whispers as they walked from room to room. Even Franny stopped her humming.

The views from the windows on either side of the living room fireplace were of the ocean. The constant sound of breaking waves echoed off the white plaster walls. There was a strong salty, seaweedy smell coming through the screen door. Jars filled with sea glass and shells covered the mantel. A seagull had perched on the chimney. It was as close as a house could be to the edge of the ocean.

CHAPTER FIVE

When they discovered that the electricity hadn't been turned on, Mr. Carlton went to the phone to call the electric company.

"Oh, that's just great!" he fumed. "Not only do we not have electricity, but the phone line is dead!"

"The realtor did tell us they lose their phone lines pretty regularly around here," Mrs. Carlton reminded him. "I don't suppose it's worth looking into on a Sunday. We'll just have to tough it out until tomorrow morning. We can go into town later for a pizza and soda. Nothing to get upset about. It's just a few little wrinkles, John."

But John Carlton did not like wrinkles. "The landlord should have seen to it that the electricity was turned on," he muttered. "It's a good thing for him the phone line is down or I'd give him a piece of my mind right now."

All the while, Jack's mind had been working overtime. "Maybe there's a psycho murderer on the loose," he suggested. "And he cut the phone lines so that later tonight he can break in when it's dark and there are no lights…"

"Jack, that's enough!" Mr. Carlton said sharply. "We've got enough things going wrong here without you making things worse. I just hope the movers get here before dark."

"Can we get pepperoni pizza?" Franny asked.

"What if the psycho guy—"

"Jack!" Mr. Carlton boomed. "What did I tell you about making up those stories? If you'd put half as much effort into your schoolwork as you do into making up this outlandish nonsense, you could be at the top of your class."

Jack shrugged. He wanted to tell his father that he didn't care about being at the top or the bottom of his class, but he knew that would only bring on another lecture.

"I don't think my kitties like staying in a house with no lights," Franny announced, cuddling two stuffed animals. "They're afraid of the dark."

"Tell your kitties that there's nothing to be afraid of," Mrs. Carlton said as she set about unpacking her collection of handmade quilts and antique oil lamps. "Electricity hadn't even been invented when this house was built, you know," she said brightly. She held up an oil lamp. "These are what the keeper would have used. And they'll give us plenty of light."

The movers did arrive in time to unload the van and set up the furniture before the sun went down. Later that night, as he was eating his pizza, Jack had to admit he liked the warm soft glow of the oil lamps, but he would have preferred the soft glow of a television's light even better.

Jack helped his father build a fire in the fireplace, and the family gathered around it. All the while, the sounds of sea gulls and the crashing of waves on the beach reminded everyone just how far they were from Iowa. Mrs. Carlton suggested a game of Scrabble to take their minds off feeling homesick. Franny was too young to know many words, so they played in teams, the women against the men.

Jack enjoyed Scrabble. He liked to think up funny words like *stooge*, *blubber*, and *blob*. His problem wasn't coming up with the words. His problem was spelling them, for after math, spelling was his least favorite subject.

"Why don't we keep a list of all the words you can't spell," his father suggested, reaching for a piece of paper. "That way you can study them tomorrow."

"Nobody else's father finds homework for them to do every time they play a game," Jack complained.

"Not everyone has a problem with spelling the way you do," Mr. Carlton reminded him.

Jack's shoulders slumped. Why did his father always have to remind him of his problems? And why did he always have to let him know what needed improvement?

"I quit," Jack said. "I'm not playing a game that I'm going to get homework from."

"John, maybe we could just forget the spelling list for tonight and enjoy the game," Mrs. Carlton suggested.

"All right, all right," Mr. Carlton said, throwing up his hands. "I just thought it would help improve his vocabulary."

Although his father had put the list away, Jack could feel

his critical eyes scanning every word he attempted to spell. As the game came to a close, Jack spelled out the word *belch*. And even though he forgot to put in the *c* and his father was quick to correct him, Jack couldn't help grinning when Franny asked what the word meant.

"I'd be happy to demonstrate," Jack said, and took another swig of soda and burped as loud he could.

"Jack!" Mrs. Carlton scolded. "Don't be rude."

"I was just trying to improve her vocabulary," Jack protested.

The women in the family finally won the game as Mrs. Carlton helped Franny to spell out the word *dent*.

"Is it Jack's Dent?" Franny asked when her mother said the word aloud.

Jack's smile suddenly faded as the memory of his best friend came rushing back.

"No, sweetie," Mr. Carlton said quickly. "It's a different dent. And I think it's time for bed now."

"You see, we can do just fine for a night without electricity," Mrs. Carlton announced as they put away the game.

"That's what this place is all about," Jack muttered as he thought about Denton in his messy house in Iowa. "Living without things—without electricity, without a phone, without TV, without friends…"

"Without Chuck E. Cheese's," Franny added.

CHAPTER SIX

Jack's bedroom was an attic room on the third floor. In the daylight the room had looked inviting, with twice the space of his old room back in Ames. There was a wall full of shelves for his games and puzzles. But now in the glow of the oil lamp, the sloped ceiling felt as if it were closing in on him, and the muffled roar of the ocean from the window sounded threatening. He glanced over at Ned, who was restlessly darting from one side of his terrarium to the other.

As Jack was getting into his pajamas, his father discovered a row of old books on one of the bottom shelves. Each night before going to sleep, Mr. Carlton read to Jack. It was a ritual they had started long ago, before Jack had learned to read himself. It had become Jack's favorite time to spend with his father. It didn't even matter what they were reading; just the sound of his father's voice and the smell of his minty aftershave somehow made Jack feel safe and warm.

"These all seem to be about things that have to do with the sea," Mr. Carlton said as he scanned the titles with a flashlight. "Here's one about building a sailboat and another all about rope knots. There's one on whale hunting and crabbing and even one on collecting shells."

"Who wants to collect shells?" Jack muttered, sitting down on his bed.

"Reading is a great way to improve your vocabulary, Jack, whether it's about shells or anything else," Mr. Carlton said. "It's never too early to be thinking of college, and a good vocabulary will make all the difference if you want to stand out."

Jack kicked the edge of his bed with the heel of his foot. Why did his dad always have to talk like a principal, even at home, even at night? Out loud, he asked, "Why do I have to stand out? Why can't I just stand normal, like everyone else?"

Mr. Carlton smiled. "People who settle for second best will never come in first place. You've got to set your sights high, Jack. You've got to reach for the top."

Jack knew that his father had done just that. Mr. Carlton often spoke of the poor family he had come from and how hard he had worked to win scholarships to college so that he could become a school principal.

"*Mysteries of the Deep*," Mr. Carlton read from the cover of another book now. "You like mysteries, Jack. Why don't you give this a try?" He laid it down on the bedside table.

"Aren't you going to read it to me?" Jack asked, surprised.

His father yawned and stretched his arms. "Oh, buddy,

I'm really beat with all this moving," he said. "Why don't you read a chapter to yourself tonight?"

Jack shrugged and tried to hide his disappointment. Everything seemed to be changing. Everything seemed to be wrong. He walked over to the window and looked out at the lighthouse.

"This really is a great room," Mrs. Carlton said as she carried in a box of clothes.

It would be a great room, Jack thought, if only Denton was here. He imagined them sitting up on his bed, talking about lizards and watching the lighthouse together.

After his parents kissed him good night and left a flashlight for him, Jack lay in his bed listening to their footsteps going down the stairs. He reached for the harmonica on his night table and blew a few notes. He felt his lower lip begin to tremble at the familiar sound.

"Good night, Dent," Jack whispered as he tucked the harmonica under his pillow. He tried closing his eyes, but he couldn't sleep. He was missing his friend too much.

Jack turned on the flashlight and tiptoed out of bed. He pulled a candy bar out of his backpack and aimed his light at the shelves along the wall. He reached for the book about rope knots and carried it back to his bed. Jack turned the pages slowly, looking at all the fancy knots with names like double diamond, cat's-paw, Turk's head, and fisherman's bend.

He wished he had some rope so he could try a few out. Jack decided that the double diamond was his favorite. He took a bite of the candy bar and read the directions for tying a single diamond. Then he studied the diagrams before moving on to the double diamond.

But without a rope it was impossible to practice. He closed the book and reached over to put it on his night table. It was then that he noticed *Mysteries of the Deep*, the book his father had left there.

Jack picked it up and ran his finger over the tiny gold anchor on the blue spine. He took another bite of the candy bar and opened the book.

The first story he read was all about a lighthouse and the ghost who haunted it. The ghost was a sea captain who had gone down with his ship and visited Davy Jones's locker. At first Jack didn't understand who this Davy Jones was and what was in his locker. But as he read on, he realized that "a visit to Davy Jones's locker" was an expression meaning someone had drowned at sea.

As Jack read about the ghost stalking its victims, he felt his heart begin to race. After he read how one keeper had thrown himself off the tower's gallery and another had jumped from a window to his death, Jack closed the book with a worried gulp.

What if Lizard Light had such a ghost? What if it wanted to stalk him? Jack considered going downstairs

and telling his parents how frightened he was, but the thought of going down the creaky old steps in the dark was more frightening than staying alone in bed.

Jack squeezed his eyes shut tight each time the beam of light from the tower fell across his bed. The light did little to ease his fears. As he listened to the old house's creaks and moans and the waves crashing on the rocks outside his window, Jack winced. He felt as if he were lying in some old sea gull's nest, perched high in the air, away from the safety of his family below. He buried his head under his quilt to hide.

Ned was hiding, too. He was wedged under his tree branch. Each time the lighthouse's rays flooded his terrarium with light, the little lizard blinked frantically. Ned's fear was different than Jack's, though. For Ned knew something Jack didn't. Ned knew that come midnight they could expect company. And midnight was only three hours away.

CHAPTER
SEVEN

Later that night, after the oil lamps had been blown out and everyone lay sleeping under quilts, a stillness settled over Neversink Cottage. It was an unearthly stillness that hung heavy in the air. Ned noticed it right away. So did Huxley, the goldfish, from his darkened bowl in the dining room.

The silence in Jack's bedroom was broken only by the restless surf outside his window and the faint clicking of the minute hand on his Mickey Mouse alarm clock. The clock sat atop an unpacked box on Jack's dresser.

It was the clicking that bothered Ned more. Each click the little lizard heard let him know that it was another minute closer to midnight. In the beam of light pouring in through the window, Ned could see Mickey's grinning face. He could also see that the minute hand was just two clicks away from meeting the hour hand at twelve. Two clicks away from midnight!

Ned flicked his tongue nervously as he eyed Jack, asleep in his bed. He tried running over a piece of lettuce in his terrarium, hoping the crunching sound would be enough to wake Jack, to warn him. It wasn't. The clock clicked again.

In a panic, Ned tried knocking his tail against the

terrarium's glass, but Jack slept on, unaware of the impending danger. The little lizard arched his back in fear as he heard the final click.

A chill breeze rushed in through the open window, and with it came the whispered words, "Still up, Lizard? Good of you to wait…"

Ned froze with terror on hearing the familiar voice and seeing the filaments of light that silently formed at the foot of Jack's bed. Once again he watched helplessly from his terrarium as the strange figure took shape before him.

A gull's sharp cry suddenly pierced the night air, and Jack's eyelids fluttered open. When he saw something flash before him, he closed his eyes, thinking it must be a dream. But when he opened them again, the apparition was still there.

It was unlike anything Jack had ever seen before, a wavy image swirling in a haze of light. But it was not a solid form, for Jack could see clear through it to the dresser on the other side of the room. As the light continued to swirl, he could hear a hollow giggle and see the flicker of an eyelash, the uncurling of fingers, the flash of white teeth!

Jack lay frozen with fear as he felt an icy finger of wind graze his bare neck. The slight scent of decaying seaweed wafted under his nose. He longed to dive under his blankets to hide. But he dared not move, for his eyes were riveted to the strange figure taking shape before him. His heart pounded in his chest as he watched the thing come closer!

Jack opened his mouth to scream, but before he could find his voice he noticed that the image was growing sharper. As the filaments of light condensed, the figure grew more defined. And suddenly Jack could see that the translucent image standing in the glow of the lighthouse was that of a boy!

He was wearing a white shirt and blue pants rolled up to his knees. He had a cloth cap perched on the back of his head, and his bare feet were covered in sand. His unkempt straw-colored hair framed a deeply tanned face that dimpled when he smiled. It was dimpling now.

It took all of Jack's courage to speak. "Wha-wha-what are you?" he stammered.

"Nathaniel Witherspoon is my name," a voice declared.

Jack bit down on his trembling lip as the boy lifted his cap from his head and nodded. Sewn onto the cap's brim was a small brass anchor-shaped button. When the tower's light shifted, the anchor, along with the boy's image, suddenly disappeared into the shadows.

"Don't come any closer," cried Jack, grabbing the flashlight under his quilt. "I've got a gun under here. And I'll shoot."

A giggle rippled through the darkness.

"Wha-what do you want?" Jack sputtered.

"I want to see who's living in my cottage," came the calm reply.

Jack switched on the flashlight and shone it in the boy's eyes. They were unblinking and blue as the ocean. Jack aimed the light lower, and the boy's mouth turned up into a sheepish grin that was so like Denton's, Jack nearly dropped the flashlight.

"What do you mean, *your* cottage?" he asked as he tightened his grip on the light.

"My father, Samuel Witherspoon, was the keeper here," the boy explained. "He built Neversink Cottage and the boathouse too, the year before I was born."

"But this house is supposed to be a hundred years old," Jack exclaimed. "That's what the realtor told my parents."

"More than one hundred years," said the boy, nodding his head. "'Twas built in 1838, to be exact."

"But that can't be!" Jack whispered. "Then that would make you..."

"Mad as a white squall," Nathaniel Witherspoon finished Jack's sentence. "For they've gone and left the light on its own. How do you expect to keep a light in order if you don't care for it every day? The brass is in want of polishing, and the glass needs washing. Mad as a squall is what I am."

43

"Are you, are you…" Jack struggled to get the words out. "Are you a ghost?" His hand trembled badly as he tried to steady the flashlight.

"Well," the boy whispered as he leaned over the bed with a wink. "I've been down for a look at Davy Jones's locker, if that's what you mean."

A sprinkling of sand fell from his sun-bleached hair onto the quilt.

Jack looked down at the sand and his mouth dropped open. It was real sand from the head of a real ghost!

CHAPTER
EIGHT

"I'm not jumping out any windows, ghost. I can tell you that right now," Jack said, clutching the quilt to his neck.

"Well, I should hope not," the young ghost replied, looking somewhat confused. "I would rather you called me by my Christian name, Nathaniel, if you please."

"And I'm not jumping off the tower, either," Jack croaked.

"Jump off the tower? Why, you'd be dashed to pieces on the rocks if you did!"

"Isn't that what you want?" Jack whispered. "Aren't you here to stalk your victims?"

"Stalk my victims?" Nathaniel Witherspoon rolled his eyes and gave out a little snort. "You know, Jack, sometimes you sound a bit daft."

"How'd you know my name?" Jack's voice had grown trembly.

"Why, I've known you were coming for some time. I've been waiting for you and your lizard."

Jack's face went white. "You were waiting for me and Ned? Why us?" he gasped. "Why don't you go and haunt somebody else?"

"I don't want to haunt anyone," Nathaniel said curtly,

as if offended by the suggestion. "I just thought that we might be able to talk."

"Talk? You just want to talk?"

"Mmm," Nathaniel murmured as he pulled the little lighthouse lamp from the box on the dresser. "You know what I find most tiresome about keeping a light? 'Tis the silence. Sometimes I long to have someone around, someone my age to talk to. Do you take my meaning, Jack?"

Jack hesitated. "I don't mean to be rude," he whispered. "But not many people want to talk to a ghost, especially when he looks all wavy and scary, the way you looked when I first saw you. And even now, it's not easy talking to somebody you can see through."

Nathaniel sighed. "'Tis true. It does cause a bit of a fright. But I don't look bad now, do I? As long as I stand still, I'm easier to look at, aren't I?"

"Sort of, but how does it work?" Jack asked. "I mean, can everyone see you?"

Nathaniel shook his head. "My spirit is tied to the light of the tower." He looked out the window and pointed to the lighthouse. "Only when its beam is shining can I be seen, and only by those I choose to see me."

"Why me?" Jack whispered as a wave of goose bumps rippled down his arms. "Why choose me?"

Nathaniel flashed him a smile. "Because you're a boy and because you're like me."

"How do you know what I'm like?" Jack demanded.

The young ghost laughed. "Isn't it enough to know that I chose you because you're special? You have a gift."

"A gift? Me? What gift do I have?" Jack spoke barely above a whisper now.

"Why, you're a dreamer, Jack," Nathaniel told him. "You're an explorer."

"But I've never been anywhere," Jack protested. "Just to Disney World once and—"

"In your mind, Jack," Nathaniel interrupted, tapping his finger on his forehead. "You've traveled great distances here, in your mind. That's your gift. And that makes you exactly the kind of boy I need."

"Need? Need for what?" Jack whispered anxiously.

Once again, the young ghost flashed the sheepish grin that was so like Denton's it caused Jack's heart to skip a beat. He watched as the ghost turned his head toward the window and pressed his sandy toe into the wooden floor.

"Red sky at morning, sailors take warning," Nathaniel said as he looked out over the waves. "And it won't be long afore the morning's come. Good talking to you, Jack…"

Suddenly, his voice began to fade and the beam of light

47

from the tower swept across the room, casting him back into the shadows. An eerie stillness followed. When the beam of light from the tower returned, Jack was stunned to find no one there.

"Hey!" Jack called in the dark. "Ghost—er, Nathaniel—where are you?" But there was no reply.

Jack pulled up his quilt and curled around his pillow. His mind was a jumble of unanswered questions.

Where had the ghost gone? Was he coming back? And what did he really want?

As he recalled the strange encounter, Jack felt a heavy drowsiness coming over him. The sounds of the sea were soothing to him now, like a lullaby. He felt himself drifting off, as if carried by a wave.

But there was one moment that haunted him past sleep and into his dreams. For Jack Carlton's mind could not let go of the image of that ghostly figure wearing his best friend's grin, or of the whispery voice repeating over and over, "You're exactly the kind of boy I need."

CHAPTER NINE

When Jack opened his eyes the next morning, the first thing he saw was a little gold anchor shimmering in the early morning light. The anchor was on the spine of the old book sitting on his bedside table. It was exactly like the one on Nathaniel Witherspoon's cap. Suddenly, his midnight meeting with the young ghost came rushing back. Jack sat bolt upright in bed.

Had it really happened? He tried to recall the ghost's translucent image and the sound of his voice. But in the bright light of morning, it seemed too fantastic to believe that he had really sat up all night talking to a ghost. And yet…

Jack called over to Ned.

"Did you see him, buddy? Was he really here? Or was I dreaming?"

Ned didn't answer, not with a blink of his eye or a flick of his tongue, for the lizard was sound asleep.

That's strange, Jack thought. Ned is always awake before I am. I wonder why he's so tired.

Jack yawned and scratched his head as his thoughts returned to the ghost. Could there really be such a thing? For Jack knew how strong his imagination was, and he knew how easily he could let himself get carried away.

Is that what happened last night? he wondered as he rooted though a box of odds and ends. Did I just go too far? He finally decided that the ghost most likely had been a dream, the strangest he'd ever had, but a dream nonetheless.

Jack pulled his old water gun out of the box, shook it, and grinned. Just enough water left inside for a few good shots. He took aim at his pillow, but then turned at the sound of a gull at the window. He shot a stream of water that hit the glass above the screen. The gull flew off as Jack walked over to the window.

He could see the ocean below sparkling as if beaded with diamonds of light. The gulls were diving for their breakfast, and in the distance, two sailboats were racing on the wind. There was no one on the beach, no one on the rocks. Jack thought about all the days he had before him, looking out over that lonely beach. Then he thought of Nathaniel, standing in the same spot, looking out over the sea.

"If I did dream you up," Jack whispered, taking a breath of the salty air, "I hope I can do it again."

He left the window and was heading back to his bed when he felt something scratchy under his bare feet. Jack held his breath as he slowly lifted his right foot from the wooden floor to find that he was standing on a small patch of sand!

"I wasn't dreaming!" Jack cried, rubbing his big toe in the sand. "He really was here, Ned, he really was!"

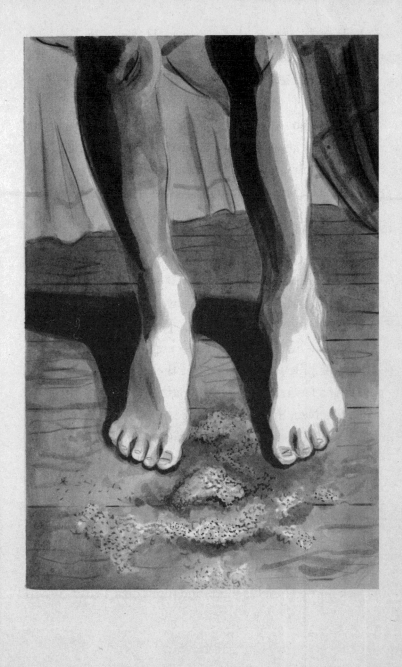

Jack raced over to the terrarium. He woke up the little lizard and placed him on the floor. Ned took one look at the sand and scurried as fast as he could in the opposite direction.

"You're right," Jack said, going after him. "It is scary to know that a ghost was in this room—but just think, Ned, we're the only ones who know he was here!"

Jack picked up the lizard and lay down on his bed with him, placing Ned on his stomach. Ned quickly curled his tail over Jack's belly button.

"The question is, will he come back? And where does he go during the day?" Jack whispered excitedly.

Ned responded with a flurry of worried blinks.

"I know, I know. It *is* spooky," Jack agreed. "I just wish Denton was here. We could really use his help." He reached under his pillow and pulled out the harmonica. He tried blowing a few notes of "Happy Birthday."

"Gosh, Ned, think about all the birthdays the ghost must have had if he's really as old as this cottage!" Jack said. His brow suddenly wrinkled. "I wonder if you can still have birthdays after you're dead?"

"JACK!" Franny yelled from the second-floor hallway. "Mom says to come down for breakfast."

"I've got to go," Jack whispered, lifting Ned off his stomach and placing him on the pillow.

Jack hurried into his shorts and threw on a T-shirt. When

he looked back down at the bed, the little lizard had bowed his head in his most pleading "Can't I come with you?" pose.

"Oh, all right," Jack sighed, slipping him into his T-shirt pocket. "But you know the 'No lizards at the table' rule. You'll have to be good and stay hidden."

Ned blinked in agreement as Jack shoved the harmonica into the back pocket of his shorts.

"And after breakfast we'll go exploring," he whispered down to Ned. "Maybe we can find some trace of the ghost. We'll check out this whole place, especially around the lighthouse."

Ned curled up into a ball in the corner of the pocket.

"Oh, come on," Jack coaxed, tapping Ned's head with his finger. "You know you love exploring as much as I do."

Jack felt a shiver down his back as he thought about what he'd just said. Hadn't the ghost told him he was an explorer? But how could the ghost know that he loved exploring? And what else did he know?

Jack was still going over these questions in his mind as he made his way down the old staircase to the kitchen. He felt the worn wooden steps under his bare feet. He thought about Nathaniel Witherspoon's feet on these very same steps, and how they were now ghost feet!

CHAPTER
TEN

On entering the kitchen, Jack stopped to stare. It seemed strange to see his family gathered around their familiar furniture in this very different room. For unlike the Carltons' big modern kitchen back in Iowa, this kitchen seemed as if it belonged to another time.

It was a cozy, quirky room, with uneven floorboards and bumpy walls. There was a handmade feeling to the space. Heavy wooden beams, notched with wooden pegs, hung from the low plaster ceiling. There was a little arched fireplace with a worn brick hearth, and two blue-painted china cabinets built into the corners on either side of it.

As Jack looked around the room, he thought of eating his breakfast here, in another year, in another century.

Bing! The microwave's bell suddenly rang. Jack turned to see it sitting on the counter. He watched as his mother opened it and took out a plate of bacon.

"When did the electricity come on?" Jack asked as Franny raced past him and dove under the table.

"About an hour ago," his mother answered, arranging the bacon on a plate. "And the phone works, too. We are officially back in modern times. And your dad went shopping this morning so we could have a nice breakfast."

"I was going to see if you wanted to come with me, Jack," his father added. "But you were still asleep. This sea air sure makes for great sleeping, eh?"

It makes for great haunting, that's what it makes for, Jack was thinking. He would have loved to tell them about the ghost. But he knew better. He knew they wouldn't believe him. He knew that his mother would smile and nod, while his father would probably give him a lecture on using his imagination in a more constructive way.

And besides, the ghost had chosen to show himself to him, not to them. Nathaniel Witherspoon would be his secret, Jack decided, his secret and Ned's.

"My mice don't like this air," a little voice complained from under the table. "It makes them sick. They like our old Iowa air better."

"Well, I'm sorry to hear that," Mr. Carlton said. "But I think you'd better sit at the table now and eat your breakfast."

"Okay, but I can't leave my mice. They're too sick," Franny said, popping up from under the table. She held up three little stuffed mice. "They have the mumps."

"Mumpy mice?" Jack rolled his eyes. "You're the only little kid I know whose stuffed animals are always sick or dying."

"If she's going to be a vet someday, she's got to practice," Mr. Carlton said, patting Franny's head.

"Hon," Mrs. Carlton called, turning to her husband, "can you help me lift a few boxes off the pile? I think our juice glasses are in the bottom box with the rest of the kitchen things."

Mr. Carlton followed his wife out into the dining room, where a mountain of boxes waited to be unpacked. Once they were gone, Jack reached for the scrambled eggs on his plate, shoved them into a napkin, and stuffed the whole thing into the pocket of his shorts. Jack hated eggs.

"I'm telling," Franny whispered with a grin.

"Please, Fran, don't," Jack pleaded.

"What will you give me if I don't?" she asked.

Jack suddenly regretted finishing off the last of his candy bar. If he didn't offer her something good, she was sure to tell on him. He thought about returning the egg to his plate but couldn't bring himself to do it.

"I'll tell you a good secret if you promise not to say anything," he whispered.

"What kind of secret?" Franny demanded.

"First you have to promise not to tell Mom or Dad about the egg," Jack ordered.

Franny's brown curls bobbed up and down as she nodded her head yes.

"It's a really big secret," Jack explained. "And you're the only one who's going to know about it—besides Ned, of course, who saw him."

"Saw who?" Franny asked as she dipped her mouse's worn pink nose into the jelly on her toast.

"The ghost," Jack whispered. "The ghost that came to talk to me up in my room last night."

Franny's dark eyes widened as she licked the jelly off her mouse's nose. "What did he say?" she asked between licks.

"He told me that he lived in this cottage more than a hundred years ago," Jack whispered. "He ate in this very room."

"At this table?" Franny gasped. "Did the ghost eat at our table?"

"No, silly, our table is new, but there was probably another table that stood right here. He could have sat where you're sitting now," Jack told her. "Maybe he even played under his table when he was little, just like you do."

Franny leaned over to look under the table. "Does he still live here?" she asked in an anxious whisper.

"No, but he *haunts* here. You see, ghosts don't live, Franny," Jack explained. "Ghosts are dead."

"He died!" Franny's voice rose to a panicky pitch as she swung up her feet and stood on her chair. "Mommy, Mommy!" she screeched. "I'm afraid!"

"What are you doing?" Jack cried. He pulled on her leg as he tried to get her to sit back down. "Be quiet, will you? What are you afraid of?"

But Franny's screeches only grew louder. "The ghost!" Franny cried. "I'm afraid of the ghost! Daddy, Daddy!"

Jack sank down in his seat as his father came rushing into the room.

"What's going on?" Mr. Carlton demanded as Mrs. Carlton hurried in behind him.

"It's Jack's ghost!" Franny howled. "He's dead under the table!"

CHAPTER
ELEVEN

"No—no—that's not what I said," Jack sputtered. "She got it all wrong. There was a ghost, but it wasn't under the table. It was in my room and—"

"How many times do I have to tell you that when you make up these fantastic stories, you are lying," Mr. Carlton said, shaking his head. "And lying is just not acceptable in this family."

"But I wasn't lying," Jack tried to explain. "This was different—"

"This was no different." Mr. Carlton's face grew pinker as his voice grew louder. "A lie is a lie, and to lie is wrong."

"John, don't get so excited. It's not good for your heart," Mrs. Carlton reminded him as she helped Franny back into her chair.

Jack stole a glance at his mother. She looked tired and disappointed, disappointed in *him*, he thought. He wished she would come over and hug him, but she turned back to the sink instead. No one spoke.

"You've got to learn the difference between right and wrong," Mr. Carlton finally said, breaking the silence. "And what you did was wrong."

Jack felt his stomach tighten, and he dug his fingernails

into the side of the table. He was wrong again. He was always wrong, even when he was right.

While Jack sat silently nibbling on his toast, the family's conversation turned to their plans for the day. Mr. Carlton mentioned that he was going to make a trip to the hardware store, and Mrs. Carlton asked him to stop at the drugstore as well.

"Mommy, after breakfast can you help me write a perspiration for my mice?" Franny asked.

"I think you mean *prescription*," Mrs. Carlton chuckled as she slid an egg from the frying pan onto Mr. Carlton's plate.

"Oh, Franny, you are such a cutie," Mr. Carlton said, his face softening into a smile. "I think you need a kiss." He leaned over and kissed Franny's cheek.

Jack felt his mouth turning down into a frown.

Why is it, he wondered, when she gets a word wrong, she's "such a cutie" and she needs to be kissed? And when I get a word wrong, I get a lecture and a list to study?

When she makes up a story about her stuffed animals being sick, Dad doesn't yell at her for lying, but when I tell the truth about the ghost in my room, he punishes me.

And why is it that she gets to bring her pets to the table and I'm not allowed to? Ned is cleaner than those old stuffed mice that she drags around everywhere.

Suddenly, the unfairness of it all weighed so heavily on Jack that he longed for someone to confide in, someone to be on his side. When no one was looking, he reached into his pocket and gently pulled out Ned and placed him under his palm, at the side of his plate.

It was a move he instantly regretted, for as his father began a lecture on responsibility, Jack felt Ned squirming under his hand. The little lizard quickly wiggled his way though Jack's fingers and scurried across the table!

Fortunately, the plastic tablecloth was the same shade of green as Ned's body. When he stood still, the little reptile almost disappeared in the sea of green plastic. Unfortunately, Ned had no intention of standing still. He was feeling frisky. He wanted to explore. And his explorations were taking him directly toward Mr. Carlton's plate!

Jack blinked in disbelief as he watched Ned race around the butter dish. Then in a moment of great reptilian strength, the tiny but mighty lizard took a running leap and hurled himself into the air, coming down dead center in Mr. Carlton's sunny-side-up egg!

Jack's mouth fell open at the sight of Ned's green head poking up out of the bright yellow yolk. Jack had never known his pet to be so bold. And he had never suspected that Ned liked eggs!

When he regained his composure, Jack did a quick

scan of the room. Mrs. Carlton had gotten up to get a glass of water, while Franny was busy covering her mice with her napkin. Mr. Carlton was saying something about the importance of following rules as he poured himself a cup of coffee.

Jack breathed a sigh of relief. No one had seen the daredevil lizard—not yet, anyway. But his relief was short-lived as he watched Mr. Carlton pick up his fork and look down into his plate.

The sight of his father about to eat his yolk-covered lizard was more than Jack could bear. He jumped up from his seat and reached over the table to scoop up Ned. As he did, he knocked over a glass of juice, soaking his sister and her ailing mice. Franny screamed, Mrs. Carlton gasped, Mr. Carlton exploded, and Jack began backing out of the room as fast as he could.

"Hold it right there!" his father commanded. "Where do you think you're going?"

"Back to my room?" Jack mumbled hopefully as he dropped Ned into his pocket.

"Not now, you're not," his father said, shaking his head. "Not after the mess you've made and the rules you've broken. You sit yourself right down there and don't move until I say so." He pointed to the window seat behind Jack. "That's where your misbehavior gets you. That, and no TV for the weekend."

Jack sank down onto the window seat, pulling his knees up to his chest. He felt the sting of tears in his eyes as he turned away from his father's angry glare.

"Just look how you've begun the day," Mr. Carlton continued. "First you lie to your sister about some ghost..."

"I wasn't lying," Jack muttered as loudly as he dared. "You can go in my room and look. You can see the sand."

But Mr. Carlton was in no mood to listen.

"Enough!" he barked. "If you're going to lie, you're going to be punished. You just think about that for a while."

"Oh, John, calm down now," Mrs. Carlton said anxiously.

"He's got to learn to think about what he's doing," Mr. Carlton snapped.

His parents' voices blurred into the background as Jack pressed his forehead to the window's bubbly glass. He choked back a sob as he looked out onto the rocky beach. He was thinking, all right, but not about lying or telling the truth. He was thinking about running outside and picking up all the rocks on the beach. He pictured himself throwing them at the windows of the cottage. In his mind, he could hear the crash of broken glass. It was loud, louder than his father's fury.

Then he thought of Denton. Denton loved rocks. He

didn't throw them, though. He polished them and labeled them and added them to his collection.

If only I could talk to Denton right now and tell him everything that happened, Jack thought. Denton would understand. He always understood. Jack bit down on his lip as he thought about his best friend, living so far away.

There's no one, he thought as he laid his hand on the old pine seat. No one who understands. No one who will listen. No one to talk to.

At that moment, his fingers felt a groove dug into the wooden seat. As he lowered his head to look, a tear rolled off his cheek and fell onto the little carving at his fingertips. It was a carving Jack recognized at once.

And with the discovery of those few etched lines, he knew there was someone at Neversink Cottage who would listen, someone he could talk to. For carved into the wooden seat was a perfect anchor, shaped exactly like the one on Nathaniel Witherspoon's cap.

Who had etched the little anchor into the seat? Jack Carlton thought he knew. And it made him smile to think he was the only one who did.

CHAPTER
TWELVE

During Jack's stay on the window seat, Mr. Carlton gave him a long lecture about "responsible pet care." When Jack mentioned how unfair it was that Franny was allowed to have her mice at the table, his father was quick to point out the difference between real animals and stuffed pets.

"Stuffed pets don't jump into your breakfast," he reminded Jack. "I could have *eaten* Ned this morning, do you realize that?" Jack thought he could feel Ned's little egg-covered body trembling in his pocket.

Later that morning, Mrs. Carlton returned to her unpacking, while Mr. Carlton and Franny left for a trip to the hardware store. Jack stayed home to clean up Ned. It was no easy task, for the little lizard had no love of water. Jack spent a long time wiping him down with a wet washcloth at the bathroom sink and drying him with a towel. Then he filled his water gun and tucked it into the waistband of his shorts.

"Come on, Ned," he whispered. "We're going on a ghost hunt."

After a quick search of the bathroom, Jack and Ned proceeded to look in every corner and cubbyhole of Neversink Cottage. Jack opened closets and cupboards. He squirted his gun behind doors and under tables. Ned raced along the woodwork and scurried behind boxes.

"Nathaniel, are you there?" Jack whispered into the fireplace in the living room. But the only reply from the blackened chimney was the echo of his own voice.

Jack decided to take his search outside. He put Ned into a small mesh cage that he had bought for him after Runt ran away. It was lightweight and easy to carry, and he wouldn't have to worry about Ned's wandering off.

Before Jack could get out the door, his mother warned him to stay off the steep cliffs and to keep close to the house. Neversink Cottage sat on a small bluff that sloped down to a rocky beach. The backyard had a tiny patch of grass that ran into a scrub wood with briar roses and wild lupines growing along its edge. But it was the front yard that interested Jack. The front yard faced the sea.

Jack made his way onto the walkway leading to the lighthouse. He stopped and stared at the sight before him. It was as different from his front yard in Iowa as any place could be. There were no trees, no flower beds, no sidewalks, no streets. There were no car radios blaring, no dogs barking, no lawn mower engines racing.

Here, the presence of the sea was everywhere. The blue-green water stretched out to meet the horizon, ocean running into sky. The smell of salty brine hung in the damp air. The roar of the breaking waves blended with the clatter of broken shells and the cries of gulls.

Jack continued down the walkway until he reached the

lighthouse. He longed to go inside, to climb the stairs up to the tower's top and stand at the windows that curved around it. He imagined the view of the sea from so high up. And he imagined Nathaniel Witherspoon standing there, at his father's side.

Jack tried to open the tower's blue-painted door, but it was locked. He tried throwing pebbles up at the little window halfway to the top, but the stones fell short.

"Hey, ghost, are you up there?" he called. The only reply was the screech of a gull.

Jack finally gave up and made his way down to the rocky beach. Once there, he sat on a long piece of driftwood and placed Ned's cage beside him. He dug his feet into the sand and wiggled his toes as he picked up a stone and turned it over. A line of salt swirled over the stone's surface. Jack wished he could show it to Denton.

"Denton would go crazy here," he told Ned. "It's like rock heaven."

Ned hung close to the wire mesh of the cage.

"And if he was here, we could make a great sand castle together," Jack said, leaning over to dig in the sand. "I know what, Ned. How about I make you a castle of your very own? You are the only lizard around, and this is Lizard Light. You should definitely have your own castle."

Jack quickly set to work digging in the sand until he had

a good-sized mound. Then he carefully placed Ned's cage on top of the mound. Soon he was adding rocks and shells to decorate the lower tiers.

The sun suddenly dipped behind a big billowy cloud, and the grayness of the sky hung over the dark water. Jack looked up from his work to see the empty shoreline, and then stared out across the white-capped waves. There were only a few fishing boats in the distance. He couldn't make out the fishermen's faces or hear their voices.

Jack thought about Nathaniel Witherspoon's complaint, how he found the "silence of keeping a light so tiresome." And Jack suddenly knew what he meant. Back home in Iowa, there were always people around. Jack could watch them walking in the park across the street from his house. He could hear the neighbors on their porches and in their yards. And there was always Denton to talk to. He wished he could talk to Denton now. He wished he could tell him all about the ghost.

Jack's lower lip trembled with anger as he thought of his father and his sermon about lying. What does he know about the truth? Jack wondered. What does he know about ghosts?

He thought about how things had changed between them lately, how they never had good talks the way they used to. His father seemed to be too busy finding things wrong with him, making him feel as if he weren't good enough. Making him feel as if his father didn't care.

If he really cared about me, Jack thought, he'd never have made us move so far away, so far…

Jack felt tears stinging his eyes as he watched the fog rolling in off the water. Soon a misty haze wrapped around the lighthouse and seemed to be swallowing up the beach. Jack could feel the clammy, salty dampness of the sea on his skin. He added another shell to the castle wall and sighed.

"There's no one around this place," he said aloud. He looked up at the top of the castle, where the little lizard was waiting patiently in his cage. "There's just you and me, Ned."

At that very moment, the lamp from the lighthouse automatically switched on and a ray of light cut through the haze. Jack twitched his nose. Ned tilted his head. The breeze suddenly carried the strong scent of decaying seaweed.

Jack was startled to see a figure walking toward them on the beach. It was moving slowly out of the mist. Jack leaned over the castle to grab hold of Ned's cage. His hand tightened around the handle as the figure drew nearer.

"It's…it's you!" Jack gasped at the sight of the familiar face grinning out of the fog. "It's really you!"

CHAPTER
THIRTEEN

A whispery voice rose over the sound of the breaking waves. "That's a fine castle you've built, but you've forgotten the moat."

Jack held his breath as the beam of light from the tower swept over the water and the translucent figure of the young ghost stepped closer.

"Lucky we had a fog roll in," Nathaniel Witherspoon said, kneeling beside the castle. "Gives us a chance to talk." He looked up at Jack. "You're not digging."

"Huh?" Jack croaked.

"For the moat," Nathaniel said. "You're not digging."

"Oh, right, the moat," Jack mumbled, and fell to his knees and began to dig.

Nathaniel Witherspoon smiled. "I had a good friend once. Someone I could talk to. Have you ever had a friend like that, Jack?"

Jack gulped as he watched Nathaniel's wavy figure and realized once again that he was having a conversation with someone who was dead, someone who had died more than a hundred years ago!

"I have a best friend like that, back in Iowa," Jack managed to whisper as he continued to dig. "I can tell him everything."

"Even your secrets?"

Jack nodded.

"My friend was like that." Nathaniel sighed. "His name was Tom Farley. He lived along Gull Cove. His father was a sailmaker on the *Marietta*, a whaling ship. Tom's father did all the fancy ropework needed on ship. He taught Tom the knots, and Tom taught me."

Nathaniel reached into his pocket and pulled out a length of rope. Jack noticed that, unlike the ghost's translucent hand, the rope appeared solid.

Suddenly, Jack remembered the book about rope knots he had read the night before. "Can you...can you make knots like the double diamond?" he asked.

"Any sailor who's worth his salt can tie that one," Nathaniel replied, walking over to a log and sitting down. "Come sit and I'll show you."

"Thanks, but—but—no need to bother..." Jack stammered, not moving. As he lowered his eyes, he could see clear through Nathaniel's leg to the log behind it!

"It's no bother," Nathaniel assured him. "Come on." He patted the log beside him.

Jack took a deep breath and got to his feet. He took a few wobbly steps toward the log and then sat down as far from the ghost as he could.

"That's better," Nathaniel said. "First I'll show you the

bowline. Every sailor needs to know that one. It's a life-saving knot. One that you can always depend on."

He handed Jack the rope, placing one end in his right hand and the other in his left hand. Then he guided Jack through the passes, carefully explaining each step.

"You see, tying knots is an art," explained Nathaniel, except that he said *art* like *ott*.

"You have a funny way of saying it," said Jack.

"'Tis you who sounds strange," Nathaniel bristled. "You talk like a landlubber."

"I talk like I'm from Iowa," Jack reminded him.

Nathaniel grunted. "And I don't suppose there's many there that know a whit about tying a sailor's knot."

"I suppose not," Jack agreed.

"Well, Tom's father knew all about such things. He knew all about nippering, pointing, snaking, and grafting for some of the more difficult knots. I'll teach you what I can. But the bowline's fairly simple."

When he was through, Jack held up the perfectly tied knot and smiled nervously. Nathaniel pointed to Ned, sitting in his cage at the top of the castle.

"What's it like to have a pet lizard?" he asked.

"Ned is the best pet a kid could have," Jack replied.

"Can I hold him?" Nathaniel asked.

On hearing this, Ned raced to the corner of his cage and curled himself into a ball.

"On second thought," replied Nathaniel, "he seems a little shy."

"He's just not used to…er…company," Jack explained.

"I have a pet who loves company," Nathaniel told him. "Would you like to meet him?"

"Well, sure, but is he…" Jack hesitated as he searched for the right words. "Is he a…"

"A rascal is what he is," Nathaniel said with a grin. "Look here, you'll see." He stood up with two fingers to his mouth and whistled.

Within seconds, the wild croak of a bird could be heard calling out of the fog. Jack turned to see a small black cloud in the distance. As it grew closer, he could see a pair of black wings flapping and a beak pointing straight for them.

Jack had never seen such a bird. Its feathers were black as midnight and yet he could see clear through them!

"Oh, my gosh!" In his surprise, Jack dropped the rope to the ground as the bird swooped down and landed on Nathaniel's shoulder. "It's a…it's a…ghost bird!"

CHAPTER
FOURTEEN

"Yes, if truth be told, old Blackbeard here has had a glimpse of Davy Jones's locker, too, haven't you, mate?" Nathaniel smiled as he held out his hand for the bird to perch on.

"Blackbeard?" Jack mumbled.

Nathaniel nodded. "Ravens are known to hold the souls of drowned sailors or dead pirates. When I met this raven, he was so crafty and so smart I knew at once he must have the soul of a great pirate, and there was none smarter than Blackbeard. So that's what I named him. We met up on the gallery, one day whilst I was washing windows. I began to feed Blackbeard crackers, and he became my instant friend. He's a scavenger, he is, and will eat near everything. Have you anything for him?"

"Well, no," Jack said, shaking his head. But his face suddenly brightened, and he reached into his pocket. "Come to think of it, I *do* have something." He pulled out the squished pieces of scrambled egg and held them in his palm. "How about this?"

The ghostly raven swooped down and plucked the bits of egg from Jack's hand. Then he spread his silky black wings and flew back up to perch on Nathaniel's shoulder.

"There now, Blackbeard, where are your manners?

How do you show your appreciation for such a treat?" Nathaniel murmured, gathering up the rope and pointing to Jack. "Why don't you take this rope and give it to my friend here?"

The bird croaked loudly before taking to the air and flying above Nathaniel's head. In the next instant he had streaked down low, grabbed the rope out of Nathaniel's hand, and dropped it at Jack's feet.

"I never knew anyone could train a bird like that," Jack marveled, picking up the rope.

"Ravens make excellent pets," Nathaniel told him as they watched Blackbeard fly out over the waves. "They're smarter than most all the other birds I know. Though they can be a nuisance if you're out hunting rabbit or wild game, for they'll pick a carcass clean afore you can skin it!" He turned back to face Jack. "Since you've got the rope in your hand, why don't I teach you the double diamond now?"

Jack nodded. His nervousness about talking to a ghost was easing as he found himself actually enjoying Nathaniel's company. The two sat back down on the log, though Jack leaned away from the ghost.

"You must know a lot about the lighthouse," Jack said as Nathaniel deftly guided him through the passes of the double diamond.

"I practically grew up in the lantern room," Nathaniel

told him. "When I was very young and too short to reach the windows, my father would lift me onto a stool so that I might look out."

"Did he let you flip the switch to turn on the lights?" Jack asked.

"Switch? Why, we had no switch!" Nathaniel laughed. "We had lamps filled with oil, is what we had. Papa taught me to trim the wicks and fill the lamps. I'd often tend to the painting and polishing as well. Papa often slept during the day after keeping watch all night."

"My dad never sleeps during the day," Jack told him. "Not even on Saturdays and Sundays. Sometimes I wish he would. Then I could just goof off like other kids get to do, instead of doing work sheets."

"I'll never forget the day Papa was sleeping and Tom and I were in the kitchen," said Nathaniel. "We landed ourselves in a peck of trouble that day."

"What happened?"

"'Twas bitter cold out, so Tom and I were staying close to the kitchen stove. We had grown tired of our knitting—"

"You were knitting?" Jack giggled. "I never heard of boys knitting."

"You mean to say you don't know how?" Nathaniel replied, looking as surprised as Jack. "Why, everyone who lived along the coast knew how to knit heads and bait pockets for the lobster pots. We were always making new pots on account of the lobster was plentiful in these parts, and so there was always knitting to be done. But as I was saying, Tom and I grew tired, so we laid our shuttles down and decided to play our favorite game. We imagined that the kitchen table was our boat and we were headed out to sea."

"So you *did* play under your table!" Jack exclaimed.

Nathaniel nodded. "It made a good captain's cabin. You see, in our game I was the captain of a brigantine and Tom was my first mate. Tom was going to show me how to tie the double diamond, but first he had to go up to the crow's nest to check on our location. I was holding the rope belowdecks when suddenly I heard him shout, 'There she blows!'"

"What did that mean?" Jack asked.

"Why, that he'd spotted a whale, of course," Nathaniel told him. "And so I reached for the broomstick to use as a harpoon, but as I was going up to the quarterdeck, I had the misfortune to knock over a can of stove black from the shelf above the stove."

Jack was so caught up in listening to the story that he leaned closer to Nathaniel, not wanting to miss anything.

"That sounds bad," Jack whispered.

"'Twas very bad." Nathaniel nodded solemnly.

"Suddenly, Tom and I were staring at a sea all right. A sea of black! For the contents of the can had splattered all over the room! 'Twas just at that moment that my father walked into the kitchen."

"Oh, no!" Jack winced. "So what did you do then?"

"I did the only thing a good sailor could do," Nathaniel told him. "I braced myself for the storm ahead."

CHAPTER
FIFTEEN

Jack's dark eyes sparkled, and he sucked in his breath. He had made up a number of good ghost stories himself in the past. But he had never in his wildest dreams imagined he'd be hearing a good story straight from a ghost! As the telling grew better, Jack felt his fears slipping away. And it wasn't long before he found himself listening to Nathaniel Witherspoon the twelve-year-old boy, rather than Nathaniel Witherspoon the more-than-one-hundred-year-old ghost!

"What happened next?" Jack asked eagerly.

"Being a keeper, my father didn't take kindly to a mess of any kind," Nathaniel explained. "He was expected to keep his house and boathouse spit clean, just like his lanterns. Papa was the best lighthouse keeper on the Maine coast, you understand. So he was very, very particular about order."

"I do understand," Jack said. "Because my dad is the same way, even though he doesn't keep a light—he keeps a school in order. He hates when our house gets messy. So what happened? Did you get the kitchen cleaned up?"

Nathaniel groaned. "Took us the better part of the day. My shirt was so black I had to turn it inside out so my father wouldn't scold me for that, too."

"What did you just say?" Jack gasped. "About your shirt?"

"I turned it inside out to hide the dirt. 'Tis an old sailor's trick, to save on washing," Nathaniel explained.

Jack thought of Denton's inside-out T-shirts and felt a tug at his heart.

"And I received the added punishment," continued Nathaniel, "of sitting on the window seat and mending nets for most of that evening. Mending nets is the worst punishment a boy could imagine. 'Tis so boring you're driven to do worse things than what you were punished for in the first place."

Jack grinned. "What worse things?"

Nathaniel returned his smile. "Carving, for one. I was sitting so long on that window seat, I began to imagine the good carvings I would do, and afore I knew it, I had my knife out. Almost without thinking, I dug the point into the seat and began to scratch a design. A perfect-looking anchor, if I do say so myself. I was right proud, but only wished that I had made it someplace else."

Jack's mouth dropped open. "It was your anchor!" he whispered. "It was really yours!"

Nathaniel grinned as he pulled on the brim of his cap. "You saw it, then? What did you think?"

"I...I thought it was great," Jack gasped. He stared at

the little anchor button on Nathaniel's cap. "And somehow I knew it was you who had made it."

"I was afraid my father would know as well," Nathaniel continued. "I spent the next few days trying to hide what I'd done by sitting on the anchor whenever he was in the room. But when the blacksmith, Stimson, came to shoe our horse, I made the mistake of showing it to his son, Clyde, who had come along with him."

Nathaniel picked up a clamshell and threw it out into the water. "I told Clyde it was a secret and that he was not to tell," he muttered. "But he didn't keep his word, that little lopsided barrel of bilge water!"

Jack couldn't hide his smile. He had never heard anyone call someone a lopsided barrel of bilge water before.

"Why, 'twas out of his mouth afore his father had even fired up his coals!" Nathaniel exclaimed. "And I was given the punishment of polishing all the brass. Still, as bad as that was, 'twas better than mending those blasted nets."

"When did you learn to tie the double diamond?"

"Oh, afore Tom went off whaling, I learned that one and most all the other knots he knew."

"Tom went whaling?"

"He had been begging to go to sea since he was so big," Nathaniel explained, holding his hand to his knee. "Finally, when he turned fourteen, his father agreed. I took our dory out to Gull Cove to see him off. Blackbeard followed me most all the way."

"What's a dory?" Jack asked.

Nathaniel shook his head. "You don't mean it? You really don't know? Why, 'tis a flat-bottomed boat, of course! You really have no sea legs, have you?"

"My legs work just fine," Jack replied, embarrassed by his ignorance. He decided not to say anything else, but his curiosity got the best of him.

"This whaling ship that Tom was on, did you get to see it?" he asked.

"Oh, yes." Nathaniel sighed. "She was a beauty, she was. All the ships built in Thomaston were."

"Didn't you want to go with Tom on the whaling ship?"

"Want to?" Nathaniel's voice dipped low as he pressed his heels into the wet sand. Jack leaned closer on the log so he could hear.

"I don't suppose there was anything I wanted more," Nathaniel continued. "But my father wouldn't hear of it. He said he needed me too much, to help keep the light.

"And so, from up in the tower, I'd watch the fine schooners and clipper ships out of Booth Bay on their way to Boston. And I'd dream myself on them. I'd see myself climbing aloft to furl a sail, or keeping watch from the crow's nest, or taking a trick at the wheel. Even after Tom came back and swore he'd never go again, I still didn't change my mind. Why, I'd trade my bed for a donkey's breakfast on board a ship any day."

"A donkey's breakfast?"

"Straw," Nathaniel explained with a smile. "Tom and the other greenies slept on straw down belowdecks. What you'd call a donkey's breakfast."

"Oh, I get it," said Jack. "But you know, there's something I don't understand. If you never made it out to sea, then how did you, well, how could you…" He hesitated, trying to find the right words.

"How did I come to pay a visit to Davy Jones's locker?" Nathaniel whispered after a long pause.

"Yes," Jack said. "How?"

"How what?" he heard a familiar voice ask.

Jack jumped to his feet and spun around in the sand to see his father coming up behind him. He heard a flapping of wings and turned back to see Nathaniel heading for the water's edge. Blackbeard had flown onto his shoulder.

"Who are you talking to out here all alone?" Mr. Carlton asked.

"Don't you see them?" Jack asked, pointing to Nathaniel and Blackbeard.

"See who?" Mr. Carlton asked.

"You don't see anyone?" Jack whispered.

"All I see are some sea gulls," Mr. Carlton replied, squinting. "Is that who you're talking to?"

"Er, sea gulls, right," Jack mumbled. "Birds are smarter than you think, Dad."

"Well, your mother doesn't think it's too smart being out here in this weather. It does look as if it might rain. Why don't we head back to the house?"

Before turning toward the cottage, Jack took one last look down the beach. There, at the water's edge, he could see what his father could not. He could see the faint outline of a pair of black wings fluttering over a boy, who was disappearing into the fog.

CHAPTER SIXTEEN

On the way back to the cottage, Jack and his father stopped at the little boathouse that stood beside the driveway. It was a small clapboard building built into the bank. Although the door was locked, they were able to look in the windows. Jack could see an old wooden boat turned on its side.

"Looks like a rowboat," Mr. Carlton remarked.

"It's a dory," Jack murmured, his face pressed to the glass pane.

Mr. Carlton stepped back from the window and stared at Jack.

"What did you say?"

"A dory," Jack told him. "You can tell by its flat bottom. They're called dories."

"And just where did you pick up that piece of nautical information?" Mr. Carlton demanded.

"Oh, I…er…" Jack hesitated as he tried to think how he should answer. "One of those old books in my room is all about boats."

Mr. Carlton smiled as they continued walking toward the house. "I'm glad to hear that you're improving your vocabulary."

Jack smiled, too. It felt good to have his father's

approval, especially after the rough morning they'd had. So good that Jack decided not to mention how he really came to learn the definition of the word *dory*.

"Now if you can only improve those math skills," his father said as he wiped the sand from his new white sneakers. "We'll have to get back to the work sheets."

Jack felt his smile dissolving into a frown. Once again, his father was letting him know what was wrong.

After lunch, Jack took out his marbles and tried to interest Franny in a game. She was dressed in her favorite skunk costume and was busy performing emergency surgery on one of her teddy bears.

Jack decided to see if his mother needed any help setting up her workshop. She had taken a little room off the kitchen that was originally a pantry. Jack helped to organize her many spools of thread and jars of colored buttons. He fingered some folded costumes in a big box.

"What's this one supposed to be?" Jack asked as he held up a large green felt jumpsuit.

"Oh, that's a new one I've been working on. I'll show you," his mother said, taking the suit from him. She carefully stepped into it and fitted a little green skullcap over her head. "Well?" she smiled expectantly.

Jack stared hard. "Well, you look like a big, round, green…" He hesitated.

"Wait a minute," his mother said, reaching into another box and pulling out a jar of face paint. She quickly dabbed some green paint over her cheeks and her nose. She turned back to Jack and grinned.

Jack cocked his head. "I still don't know," he said.

"A lima bean!" his mother cried. "Don't I look like a lima bean?"

"Oh, yeah, I guess," Jack agreed. "Now that you mention it."

"Jen," Mr. Carlton said, rushing into the workroom, "I need the ironing board." He reached behind some boxes and lifted it out.

"Oh, John, you're not going to iron now, are you?" Mrs. Carlton sighed.

Mr. Carlton explained that Mr. Kroll, the superintendent of schools, had called earlier and said he would be dropping by that evening to welcome the Carltons to the neighborhood. Mr. Carlton set up the ironing board in the hopes of removing all the family's wrinkles.

"Jen, this is the superintendent of schools coming to meet us," Mr. Carlton exclaimed. "First impressions are very important."

He pressed his pants and Franny's sundress, and even insisted on giving Jack's T-shirt a "once-over."

"John, what about the pillows on the couch?" Mrs. Carlton suggested. "They look kind of wrinkly."

Mr. Carlton shot a worried look into the living room.

"I'm just kidding!" Mrs. Carlton cried, taking the iron out of his hand. "Don't you think you're overdoing it? We did just move in yesterday. Surely Mr. Kroll knows that and expects a bit of a mess."

"He's my boss, Jen. And I don't want anything to go wrong in this first meeting."

Franny came and stood at the workroom door, her black-and-white tail hanging down behind her.

"I want you kids on your best behavior tonight," Mr. Carlton said. "And, Franny, after supper you can change into this." He held up her dress.

"But I don't want to wear that," Franny protested. "I'm a skunk, and skunks don't wear dresses."

"I know what you mean," Mrs. Carlton said, shaking her green-capped head. "I'm a lima bean, and lima beans don't wear dresses either. But tonight we lima beans and skunks must pretend to be ladies. Why don't we look through this box and see if we can find some special ribbon for your hair, something to match your dress?" She handed Franny a big box of ribbons.

"Remember your manners," Mr. Carlton continued. "Smile, say hello, and be sure to answer if Mr. Kroll asks you anything. Your behavior is a reflection on the whole family. This visit is very important."

A little later, while he was in the bathroom, Mr.

Carlton called out that the zipper on his pants had stuck. Mrs. Carlton told him to bring them out and she would have a look at it.

Just then, the doorbell rang. Jack and his mother stared at each other. They weren't expecting company yet. Mrs. Carlton hurried into the living room. It wasn't until she opened the door and stood face-to-face with Mr. Kroll, the school superintendent, that she remembered her lima bean costume. Her hand flew up to her green hat just as Mr. Kroll was apologizing for his surprise visit. He'd been driving by and thought he'd drop in early, he explained.

As Mrs. Carlton stepped aside to welcome him in, Mr. Carlton barreled into the living room—in his striped boxer shorts! He stood frozen in the doorway as his pants, with their broken zipper, swung from his forearm. Franny's little skunk ears peeked out from behind him.

Jack looked at Mr. Kroll, whose mouth had dropped open. He knew this was not the first impression his father had hoped to make.

Still, Jack fought back a smile. For once, *he* wasn't the cause of the trouble! Mr. Carlton raced for the bedroom to change, while Mrs. Carlton tried to explain their unusual appearances. Mr. Kroll fake-smiled and nodded his head. Suddenly, a beefy-looking boy with curly white-blond hair materialized from behind him. Jack hadn't even seen him come in.

"Mr. Kroll, I'd like to apologize and introduce you to my family," Mr. Carlton said when he returned, fully dressed. He was talking in his most formal voice.

Mr. Kroll shook all their hands and then introduced "my one and only son, Joshua."

Mr. and Mrs. Carlton smiled. Franny smiled. Jack smiled. Joshua Kroll looked at Franny and made a face. Jack stopped smiling. He instantly disliked Joshua Kroll.

"We're happy to welcome you to the community," Mr. Kroll said, squinting. "It's a tiny bunch. In a small community such as ours, you look out for each other. Everyone knows how to get along here in Minty."

Mr. Kroll doesn't sound like a landlubber, Jack thought. His accent was like Nathaniel's.

"I'm sure we'll fit in just fine," Mr. Carlton said stiffly. Jack could hear the anxiety in his father's voice. He sounded like a nervous landlubber.

Later, as the grownups sat down for a cup of coffee in the living room, Jack and Franny returned to the kitchen. Joshua followed them in. Jack picked up his bag of marbles and began to take a few out.

"Can I play?" Joshua asked, staring at the marbles.

Jack winced. He knew it would be rude to say no. "I guess so," he muttered.

Joshua stood waiting. He pulled on Franny's tail. She instantly retreated under the table with her teddy bear. Jack dropped a number of marbles into Joshua's chubby little hand. Joshua grinned and tried to make a shot, but he ended up just throwing the marble across the floor. He seemed to like this better than shooting, and he especially liked throwing marbles under the table, where Franny was playing.

"Ouch!" Franny cried when a marble hit her leg.

Joshua laughed and threw another.

"Hey!" Jack said, turning to face him. "What are you doing? You could hurt her."

But Joshua just grinned and threw another marble, this time hitting the table. Jack reached over, trying to grab the remaining marbles out of Joshua's hand. "That's not what marbles are for," he said.

"I know what marbles are for," Joshua declared, grabbing a marble and throwing it at Franny's teddy bear. Luckily, the patient was unconscious due to the operation, but the doctor was not.

Franny let out a yelp and began to cry. Joshua started to laugh.

"Why you little lopsided barrel of bilge water," Jack fumed.

"Lopsided barrel of what?" a deep voice asked.

Jack spun around to see his father standing in the doorway. His face had gone white. Beside him was his boss, Mr. Kroll, the superintendent of schools. Mr. Kroll's face was red and growing redder. No one was smiling.

CHAPTER SEVENTEEN

"Lopsided barrel of bilge water! That's what you call the superintendent's one and only son!" Mr. Carlton cried after Mr. Kroll and Joshua had gone. "Where do you come up with these things? Do you sit up at night thinking of ways to embarrass me? Do you wonder why I have heart trouble?"

"Now, John, he was just protecting his sister," Mrs. Carlton reminded him.

"Oh, great, well, I hope he can figure out a way to feed her while he's at it. Because if I don't keep this position, we're out of luck. Do you realize I met my boss today in my underwear? I had to introduce my wife the lima bean and my daughter the skunk! And to top it all off, my son, the only normal-looking one in the bunch, calls his son a lopsided barrel of bilge-something-or-other!"

"Let's watch some TV. It'll take your mind off things," Mrs. Carlton suggested. She nodded for Jack to leave the room.

Jack's shoulders slumped as he dragged himself out to the back porch. Once again he had gotten it wrong, even though he thought he was doing right. And once again he had let his father down. How could he ever be the kind of son a principal should have? How could he ever manage to be that perfect? He just couldn't. He knew it and his father knew it.

As he sat thinking these things over, he kicked over an old bucket just for something to do, and a piece of old clothesline fell out. Jack picked up the rope and brought the two ends together. Before he knew it, he was making the passes that Nathaniel had taught him. When he was through, he had a perfect bowline! Jack was so excited that he tried the double diamond. Soon he was so busy practicing different knots, he forgot about feeling like a failure.

When his mother called him to come and get ready for bed, Jack shoved the rope into his pocket. He didn't want anyone to see it. He wanted it to be his secret, his and Nathaniel's.

Mr. Carlton didn't read Jack a story that night. He didn't even come up to tuck him in. Jack wasn't surprised when his mother tried to make an excuse for him. "Dad is just a little tired tonight," she said, reaching over to stroke Jack's hair. "Your father loves you very much. You know that, don't you, Jack?" she whispered.

Jack felt a heaviness in his chest, an ache that welled up at his mother's words. He shrugged and turned his head away.

"You have a wonderful imagination, Jack," she continued, "and I think you get that from my side of the family.

Your Uncle Quentin was always a great storyteller. And when he was young like you, he was always getting into trouble because of his stories. It wasn't that he meant to do wrong, it was just that he was seeing the world in a very different way."

"Was his dad always punishing him?" Jack asked, feeling a sob deep in his throat.

Mrs. Carlton sighed. "Your grandfather was very worried about Uncle Quentin, worried that he wouldn't be able to make it in the world. So, yes, he was hard on him, but it was only out of worry. And that's why Dad gets so upset with you, Jack. It's because he loves you so much." She leaned over and kissed Jack's forehead. "And you remember how Uncle Quentin promised to take you out on his boat? Well, he called to say that he'll be up in a few days. So get some sleep now so you'll be ready to sail."

Though the heaviness was still in his chest, Jack was glad his mother had come up. He thought about his Uncle Quentin and wished *he* were his dad instead. He also wished Uncle Quentin would come sooner.

Later that night, as the golden glow of the lighthouse brushed over his quilt, Jack fingered the rope hidden under his pillow beside his harmonica. He pulled out the harmonica and played a few notes of "Happy Birthday." He instantly thought of Denton and wished that he could somehow show him his bowline. But he knew that was impossible. How could he share anything with Denton, now that he was hundreds of miles away?

His thoughts turned to Nathaniel, and he realized that Nathaniel Witherspoon was the only friend he had. But did he have him? For a ghost wasn't like a normal friend, someone you could call up on the telephone. What if he didn't come tonight? What if he never came again?

"Please, Nathaniel," Jack whispered as he watched the lighthouse's beam from his window. "Please come back. Just to talk, just to talk."

Long after his parents had gone to sleep, Jack and Ned were still up, reading in bed by flashlight. To help them stay awake, Jack had laid in a supply of chocolate chip cookies, raisins, and lettuce under his bed. The lettuce was for Ned. Jack had also taken a stack of the old books from the shelf and dumped them onto his quilt.

Jack spread one of the books open on the bed now so that Ned could walk over the pages. The book was called *At the Edge of the Sea*. Ned liked walking over the pictures of periwinkles, mussels, and sea stars.

"Did you hear something?" Jack suddenly whispered.
Ned blinked.

Jack aimed the flashlight around the room. "Is that you, Nathaniel? Are you here?" he called hopefully. "Look, I did the bowline, just like you showed me." He pulled the rope out from under his pillow.

But there was no one there to see it, no one besides Ned. Jack dropped the rope back on the bed with a sigh. He fed Ned another piece of lettuce and took another bite out of his cookie. Then he opened a book called *Come On Board*. It was all about boating and boat maintenance.

"Someday I'm going to take a boat like that out," Jack whispered as Ned hurried across a picture of a sailboat. "And you can come with me.

"'Balance is everything,'" Jack read aloud from the book. "'A good sailor has to adjust his weight in the boat as nimbly as a ballet dancer.' Gee, Ned," Jack joked. "Looks like we might have to get you a tutu!"

Ned was not amused. He scurried off the page and onto the quilt. Jack picked up a heavy book about whaling ships. He turned to a page about the barnacles that collected on the bottom of the vessels.

"'After a long voyage the captain gave the order to *careen the ship*,'" he read aloud. "'This meant that it was to be heaved over on its side so the barnacles could be scraped off. Desperate sailors, stranded at sea, have been known to dive under their vessels to scrape the barnacles off for a meal.' Yuck," Jack said as he nibbled on a cookie. "How'd you like to eat barnacles, Ned?"

But Ned was not listening. He had curled up beside

Jack's pillow and fallen asleep. Jack yawned and looked back down at his book. He felt his eyelids growing heavy.

"I bet those barnacles tasted pretty bad," Jack mumbled as he leaned his head back onto the pillow. He felt his eyes beginning to close when a bright beam of light flashed before him and a cool seaweedy breeze rushed up his nose.

"You'll be growing barnacles on your stern if you sit in that bed all night," a familiar voice whispered.

Jack's eyes opened wide to see Nathaniel Witherspoon stepping out of the beam of light.

"You came back!" Jack grinned a nervous grin. As much as he had hoped to see Nathaniel, it was still unsettling to be talking to a ghost. Jack quickly reached for the rope lying at the foot of his bed. "Look what I made," he said, holding it up before him.

"You've been practicing without me." Nathaniel smiled as he fingered the bowline Jack had made. "Good job."

Jack felt his face flush with pride.

"Would you like to learn another? How about the cat's-paw?"

"Sure," Jack replied.

Nathaniel set to work making a large loop in the rope.

"I was wondering," Jack said as he nervously twisted a frayed string on his quilt. "When you said I was the kind of boy that you needed…just what do you need?"

There was a long silence as Nathaniel continued to work the rope.

"I need someone I can depend on, Jack," he finally answered, raising his deep blue eyes. "Can I depend on you?"

"Uh, well, sure, I guess, but depend on me for what?" Jack answered.

"Did you know that every brigantine, every schooner, every tender that traveled up or down this coast depended on our light?" Nathaniel boasted. "Between the fog and the rocks along Gull Cove, it took a skilled captain to guide his ship. And they often couldn't do it without our light. Every day before sunset, my father climbed the stairs of the tower to light the lamps. And every night at midnight, he trimmed the wicks or put in fresh ones. Not until sunrise did he extinguish the flame. My father's light never let them down. My father was the best keeper on the Maine coast."

"Yeah, you said that last time we talked," Jack reminded Nathaniel. "But getting back to what you said about depending on me, I was wondering what—"

"Tell me something, Jack," Nathaniel interrupted, a twinkle coming into his eyes. "Have you ever been up in a lighthouse before?"

"Well, no, I haven't," Jack admitted.

"Would you like to have a look?"

"Sure, that would be great sometime."

"How about now?"

"Now?" Jack's eyebrows shot up. "You mean *right* now?"

"I don't see why not."

"But the lighthouse is locked," Jack protested.

"Not for long." Nathaniel grinned as he held up a small brass key and handed it to Jack.

"Oh, I don't think so," Jack whispered, looking down at the key in his palm. "You see, I'm not allowed out of my room after bedtime."

"Ever see a shooting star fall into the ocean, Jack?" Nathaniel whispered as he looked out the window. "Now there's a sight no boy should miss."

"I guess that would be something to see," Jack agreed.

"It's a starry night out there tonight," Nathaniel sighed. "You could see most all the stars in the sky from up in the tower, enough stars to fill your dreams for the rest of your life."

Jack stepped up to the window and looked out to see the white tower glowing in the moonlight.

"I don't suppose it would hurt to have a quick look, but my father would kill us if he found out," he said under his breath.

"He can only kill one of us," Nathaniel reminded Jack with a wink. "And besides, he'll never know. We'll be out and back afore he wakes up, trust me. You do trust me, don't you, Jack?"

Jack stared hard at the boy who stood before him, a boy who had been dead for more than a hundred years. And slowly, silently, Jack Carlton nodded his head yes. Seconds later, flashlight in hand, he was following the young ghost out the door.

CHAPTER
NINETEEN

As if in a dream, Jack followed Nathaniel down the darkened stairway. Tiptoeing past his parents' bedroom, he glanced in through their open door. He could see his mother's closed eyes as the light from the tower swept over the bed. He could hear his father snoring.

Jack didn't imagine there were any stars in his father's dreams. He supposed that his father's dreams were full of perfect test scores and wrinkle-free pants. Jack hurried after Nathaniel, who was waiting at the front door.

Once outside, Jack stopped to stare. In the moonlight, the beach had an unearthly look about it, as strands of rockweed and crinkly green sea lettuce twisted around speckled gray stones. Bleached white periwinkles mingled with the deep blue of mussel shells. Rising above a jagged ledge was the lighthouse, a glistening white beacon topped with a golden light.

The breeze whipped Jack's thin striped pajamas around his legs as he followed Nathaniel down the walkway leading to the lighthouse.

"We never locked it when my father was keeper," Nathaniel muttered as Jack fitted the key into the lock. "Have you got it, then?" he asked.

Jack nodded as he pushed the door open with a loud creak.

"Go on," Nathaniel coaxed. "Go on inside."

Jack turned his flashlight on Nathaniel's face, and he could see the young ghost grinning that familiar grin. "Go on," Nathaniel whispered. "We haven't all night."

Jack shone the light back on the opened door. He took a deep breath before stepping into the darkened lighthouse. The smell of fresh paint and turpentine instantly tickled his nose. He could feel the damp closeness of the tower, as if the clammy breath of the sea had been trapped in its thick stone walls. A wave of goose bumps raced up his legs as he walked barefoot across the cold brick floor.

"They've gone and painted the steps the wrong color again," Nathaniel exclaimed as he walked over to the staircase. His voice echoed off the tower walls. Jack tried to steady his trembling hand as he shone his flashlight up the twisted stairway in the center of the tower.

"We always painted them gray," Nathaniel grumbled. "It was regulation."

Jack shone the light over a long empty shelf that hung from one wall.

"And Papa always kept his hurricane lamp there," Nathaniel pointed out. "Along with a compass and a skull he found washed up on shore as they were building

the tower. But the people from the museum came out and carried them off. Doesn't seem the same without Old Pete."

"Old Pete?" Jack whispered, unable to hide the nervousness in his voice.

"Papa named the skull Old Pete," Nathaniel explained. "Papa liked to say that Old Pete was a reminder to us all of how the sea can claim us. He said every lighthouse should have its own skull."

Jack suddenly imagined Old Pete's empty eye sockets staring through him, and he felt his knees grow weak. "You know, I think I'd better get back to my—my—my room now," he stammered.

"Without having a look from the top?" Nathaniel cried, starting up the winding staircase. "Why, you can't miss that."

Jack took a deep breath and placed his foot on the bottom step, but hesitated. It was such a long way up to the top, a long way in the dark with thoughts of Old Pete's empty eye sockets to haunt him.

"Don't be worrying about the skull," Nathaniel called, as if reading his mind. "He's long gone. Come on up now."

"There sure are a lot of steps." Jack's quivery voice echoed in the darkness as he placed his foot on the second step and started to climb.

CHAPTER
TWENTY

"One hundred and two steps to be exact." Nathaniel's voice echoed down the stairwell. "I should know, as I had to climb them every day. Seems like a thousand and two when you're carrying ten gallons of whale oil on a yoke! Can you believe those museum people took even the old wooden yoke I used to wear? I could carry five gallons on each end, but in truth I don't miss seeing it."

Jack tried to imagine what it would be like to be walking up the narrow stairway with ten gallons of whale oil hanging on his shoulders. He stopped and watched the young ghost at the little window halfway up the staircase.

"They always leave this one spotty," Nathaniel muttered, wiping the pane with a rag from his pocket. Then he continued up the stairs. Jack stopped at the window to look out. In the moonlight he could see Neversink Cottage snuggled against the bluff.

"Keep coming, Jack, you're almost to the gallery," Nathaniel called down to him.

Jack looked up to see Nathaniel's translucent figure standing before a narrow door. Beyond him, farther up, the bright beam of the automatic light flooded the tower's lantern room. Jack kept climbing. When he reached the gallery door, Nathaniel stood beside him on the landing and nodded for him to go through it. Jack lifted the iron latch and pushed the door open. A cool breeze swept his hair back as he stepped through the doorway. The sound of the waves breaking on the shore echoed from far below.

Jack grabbed for the iron railing as he nervously stepped along the gallery's walkway. He looked out at the dark waters of the ocean. It was a long way down.

Jack gripped the railing tighter. "We're so high up!" he cried, his voice carried off on the wind.

"Yes, 'tis a long way to the bottom," Nathaniel agreed, coming up to him. "But don't be looking down, Jack. Look out there."

Jack looked up to see a glittering sky hung over a calm sea, and he felt his breath catch in his throat. He had never seen anything quite like it. It wasn't like a painting, or a movie, or a page in a book. Rather, it was a great living, breathing beauty. It was the majesty of sky meeting sea, with starlight and sea foam mingling to make a magic so vast in its grandeur, he was awed into silence. Neither he nor Nathaniel spoke for a long while. They simply stood and stared.

"My father would call such a sky a sailor's delight," Nathaniel finally whispered. "He loved to stargaze on his watch. Look, there's the North Star," he said, pointing to a bright star overhead. "And look at those, there. That's the Big Dipper."

"I see it! I see the Big Dipper!" Jack cried excitedly. He turned to Nathaniel. "You know a lot about the stars."

"Stargazing and weather watching are second nature to those that keep the lights. Papa taught me all about the constellations."

"You must be really proud of your father."

"Why shouldn't I be?"

"Oh, no reason," Jack answered quickly. "It's just that lately my dad and I haven't been getting along very well."

"Aren't you proud of him?" Nathaniel asked.

Jack frowned. "Proud of my dad? Oh, it's not that." He lowered his eyes to the railing. "It's more like he's not proud of me. You see, being a school principal means that you have to set an example. At least that's what my dad is always saying. And I guess as a principal's son I set a pretty bad example. I could never be as perfect as he is."

"Well, you tie a tidy knot," Nathaniel said, pulling the rope out of his pocket. "And I'd wager you'd make a fine sailor."

"Who, me?" Jack croaked.

"Yes, you. Look how easily you took to handling the rope. I'd wager you'd take to handling a set of oars just the same."

"I don't know. I've never tried. There was no one to teach me back in Iowa. My father doesn't know anything about boats."

"You don't have to learn everything from your father,"

Nathaniel pointed out. "And maybe there are things that you are better at than he. Things that you could teach him."

Jack's dark eyes widened. He looked down at Neversink Cottage, sitting so far below them. It had never occurred to him that there was anything he could do better than his father.

"You'd make a fine sailor," Nathaniel assured him. "All you need is to try."

"I would like to learn," Jack admitted as he watched a large white-capped wave crash onto the sand.

"What about tonight?" Nathaniel suggested.

"Tonight?" Jack gasped.

"Why not?" Nathaniel shrugged. "You've got the dory, and—"

"What dory?"

"The one in the boathouse," whispered Nathaniel, pointing to the building below.

"But it's locked," Jack reminded him.

"And you've got the key," Nathaniel said with a wink.

"Are you saying what I think you're saying?" Jack exclaimed, looking down at the brass key in his hand.

"I'm saying that I know a sailor when I see one," Nathaniel replied. "Why, I took a skiff out on my own long afore I was your age. You've got to find your sea legs sometime, Jack. Besides, look for yourself." He leaned over the railing. "There's a full moon, and the sea's running smooth as silk. Perfect conditions for a moonlight cruise."

Jack leaned into the railing. His head was suddenly swimming. How would he ever find out if he really could be a good sailor if he didn't try? And what would it be like to be really good at something his father knew nothing about? Wouldn't it be worth the risk to find out? But what if he failed? What if he sank the boat? And worse, what if he ended up like Nathaniel, paying a visit to Davy Jones's locker?

The young ghost's voice was suddenly in his ear, low and velvety smooth. "There's something about setting out on the sea in the moonlight," he whispered. "To be gliding over liquid silver under a starlit sky, away from the mainland, away from all of their straight-lined streets and square-cornered houses.

"You've a sailor's soul, Jack, just like me. You were meant for adventure, for the curve of the wave. Come with me to the boathouse. Come with me on the sea…"

His heart pounding, Jack looked down at the shimmering water. He took a gulp of the salty night air. "Yes," he whispered into the darkness. "I will come. I will."

CHAPTER
TWENTY-ONE

No sooner had Jack agreed to go out on the sea than Nathaniel left the gallery and started down the old stairway. Jack could hardly keep up with him as he raced down the 102 steps. Around and around, down and down, into the darkness. It was all Jack could do to stop himself from toppling over in his dizzy flight.

He came at last to the tower's opened door, where he stood trying to catch his breath. Jack could see Nathaniel running down the walkway, and he took off after him. At the end of the wooden ramp, he jumped onto the sand and followed Nathaniel, running down the beach. Jack could feel his heart pounding in his chest as the echo of the ocean roared in his ears. He had never been out alone at night and never so close to the sea.

Jack looked back at Neversink Cottage, sitting snug and safe on the shore, holding his entire family. He felt his resolve weakening as he pictured himself sitting up in bed, reading with Ned. Then he thought of his mother's bright smile as she lit an oil lamp, and of Franny with her sparkly Band-Aids, trying to write "perspirations." He recalled the sound of his father's voice, reading him a story. And he suddenly felt the urge to go back.

Jack was turning in the sand, back toward the cottage, when he heard Nathaniel call, "Hurry, mate. The wind is with us."

As homesick as he was, Jack felt a shiver of excitement at the sound of this. He loved the way Nathaniel had called him "mate," as if they were sailors already. And he suddenly remembered his father's remark about Jack's being responsible for his heart attack. It stung him to think that maybe all his failures had caused his father's illness. Maybe he could turn it all around. Maybe he could do something right after all.

Jack looked up to see Nathaniel racing ahead, his shirt billowing behind him like a ghostly white sail in the wind. Meanwhile, the full moon hung over the sea as the stars shimmered above the waves. Jack stepped away from the cottage once again, away from the safety of the land, to follow the young ghost's footsteps.

"We'll have to be quick if we want to return with the tide," Nathaniel whispered once they reached the boathouse. Jack fitted the brass key into the lock. Together the two pulled open the big white door and looked in. The dory was on her side. Nathaniel reached for the oars, which were hanging on a wall. He laid them in the boat and told Jack to grab hold.

"We're lucky she's a lightweight," Nathaniel said as they lifted the dory up and out of the boathouse.

Jack winced under the weight of the boat. "You call this light?" he groaned.

"I guess you need to find your sea arms as well as your sea legs," Nathaniel laughed.

When they finally reached the water's edge, Jack leaned over the gunwale to catch his breath.

"Lesson number one," Nathaniel instructed. "Always have your oarlocks in place and your oars ready afore you leave shore. That way, if the wind's against you, you're in a better position to fight it. It's the westerlies that we have to fight in this cove."

Jack didn't like the sound of this. Nathaniel hadn't mentioned fighting anything when he first spoke of "a moonlight cruise" back in the lighthouse. He watched nervously now as Nathaniel positioned the oarlocks and picked up the oars.

A small wave suddenly broke at their feet, drenching the bottom of Jack's thin pajama pants. The water was icy cold and sent a shiver rippling all through him.

"Hurry! Get in," Nathaniel shouted. "I'll take the stern. You sit there." He pointed to the rowing seat.

With the surf pounding in his ears and his heart racing in his chest, Jack climbed into the boat. He grabbed hold of the oars as Nathaniel put one foot in the boat, gave a hard shove, and jumped in.

"Pull, pull!" Nathaniel cried as they caught an outgoing wave.

Jack dipped the oars into the water and pulled. It was harder than he had imagined, and at first he wondered if he'd be able to do it at all. He felt his palms burn as he gripped the oars tighter. A red button on his pajama shirt popped off and into the boat as his chest expanded and his arms strained to drag the oars through the water.

"Take her out! Hurry! Afore she turns turtle!" shouted Nathaniel as they mounted a giant white-capped wall of water. Jack felt the adrenaline pumping through him. The wave swelled and lifted them higher. The back of his throat stung from the salty air he was gulping down in anxious gasps. His panic rose with each swell they encountered.

Would they clear the next wave before it broke? And what if they didn't? What if they did "turn turtle"? Jack looked over the edge of the boat, unable to see the bottom.

"Nathaniel," he cried. "What about life jackets? Shouldn't we be wearing life jackets?"

In the glow of the lighthouse, he could see Nathaniel's lips slowly curve into a smile until his white teeth glistened in the moonlight. And as the boat lurched up and then came crashing down off the top of a wave, Jack heard a low chuckle that burst into a laugh. It was a ghostly laugh that echoed off the dark waters and up into the velvety night, a laugh that took Jack's breath away and filled him with horror. For on hearing it, he suddenly understood the real danger he had placed himself in.

He understood that Nathaniel Witherspoon needed no life jacket, not now, not for the rest of eternity. What Nathaniel Witherspoon needed was a friend, a friend to fill the loneliness of more than a hundred years' longing, a friend who would never leave him.

As the little dory dipped and danced over the rippling surf, carrying them farther and farther away from the shore, Jack shuddered to think that he was to be that friend. He felt his blood run cold as Nathaniel's voice sailed over the wind.

"Don't worry, Jack. I'll see that you won't need a life jacket, not now, not ever again."

CHAPTER
TWENTY-TWO

Jack fought hard not to cry. "What do you mean I won't need a life jacket?" he whispered, sitting as far back in his seat as he could.

Nathaniel flashed him a sheepish grin, and Jack shuddered.

It's that grin, he thought frantically now. That's why I trusted him. He smiles just like Denton! But he's not Denton. Nathaniel Witherspoon is dead! How could I forget that? He's dead and he wants me to be dead with him!

"Don't worry," Nathaniel called to him, still smiling. "Everyone's a bit jittery on their first trip."

"Trip?" Jack demanded. "Trip to where? Where is it we're going that I won't need a life jacket?"

"What are you talking about?" Nathaniel cocked his head, perplexed. "You won't need a life jacket on account of you'll be such a good sailor you won't need to swim."

"A ghost sailor?" Jack whimpered. "Did you say a ghost sailor?"

"A *good* sailor," Nathaniel called over the wind. "What's all this about being a ghost?"

"Isn't that why you got me out here?" Jack asked in a

quavery voice. "Aren't you hoping to take me for a visit to Davy Jones's locker?"

"If you're ever to make that voyage, it's not for me to navigate," Nathaniel assured him.

Jack took a deep breath and relaxed his grip on the oars. "Then you're not trying to get me drowned?"

"Drowned!" Nathaniel hooted. "Why, it's the one thing that I'm trying to see that you don't do! Look here, Jack, you've got a good handle on the oars. If you can get her back in as smoothly as you took her out, there's no reason for you to get wet at all."

Jack sighed with relief. "I'm sorry, Nathaniel," he apologized. "I guess I just let my imagination run away with me."

"What you need to imagine now is the rocks that edge the cove," Nathaniel warned. "They're there, just under that smooth line of surf." He pointed to the right of the tower. "You'll have to keep her away from them. Backstroke with your left oar to turn her around."

Jack did as Nathaniel ordered, and the dory obediently turned.

"Hey! Look, she's turning," Jack shouted. "She's turning!"

"She's a sweet one, she is." Nathaniel's dimples were showing as he pulled on his cap. "Of course, they aren't all this sweet. Every dory has its own personality. Some are testy and fidgety, while others take to the surf like dancers. Some glide along gracefully, while others sulk and pout and fuss with every wave."

"I'd say this one is a dancer," Jack decided. "Hey, Nathaniel, did you ever make a ship in a bottle?"

Nathaniel frowned. "No, that was my father's fancy. I'd rather be sailing a ship than squeezing one into some whiskey bottle." He dipped his hand into the water and skimmed the foam from a wave. "What's it like to live so far from the sea?" he asked.

Jack leaned back in his seat and looked out over the dark water.

"Well, it's different. We don't have anything as big as an ocean. The biggest thing we have is the county pool. I used to be afraid of its deep end, but not anymore. And to tell you the truth, when we first started out, when I was still on the beach, I was so afraid of the ocean I was thinking of turning back."

"There's no shame in that," Nathaniel told him. "Any old salt can speak of such fear. You'd be foolish *not* to be afraid. You have to respect the sea, Jack, and that includes fearing her. For 'tis a mighty force that can swallow an entire ship in one frothy gulp."

Jack gulped himself at the thought of this. And he wondered if that had been Nathaniel's fate. Had he, too, been swallowed up in a frothy gulp?

"What about you, Nathaniel?" he asked timidly. "Were you ever afraid?"

"There were plenty of times as I sat up in the lantern room, watching a storm brewing, that I wished I was farther inland," Nathaniel admitted. "From that first whisper of a gale you can feel your courage lessen, because you know what's to follow. 'Tis not the wind you're afraid of, but what's behind it. For one gale can hook on to another and another, and before it's through, thousands of miles of ocean have been churned into a force that can swallow a ship as easily as take down a tower. For me the misery was the whispering just before the storm."

"Did many ships wreck on your shore in a storm?" Jack asked.

Nathaniel nodded.

"And did your father have to row out to save the survivors?"

There was no reply to this, and at first Jack thought that maybe Nathaniel hadn't heard him. He began to repeat the question when Nathaniel stopped him.

"My father was the best keeper on the Maine coast," he said with a defiance that surprised Jack.

"I never said he wasn't," Jack protested. "I was just asking…"

Nathaniel threw up his hand to silence him.

"When I tell you that my father was the best keeper on

the Maine coast, that is true. He was, until my mother's death, that is. Then he…he…"

Jack leaned forward as Nathaniel's voice grew lower. "In truth, he became the worst thing a keeper could be."

"What's that?" Jack asked.

"A coward!" Nathaniel said hoarsely, his blue eyes flashing in the moonlight.

A wave suddenly slapped against the boat, shaking Jack out of his surprised stupor.

CHAPTER
TWENTY-THREE

Jack licked the salt from the ocean's spray off his lips as the beam from the tower washed over Nathaniel's troubled face. The crash of broken shells echoed as a wave hit the beach. Jack waited for Nathaniel to continue, not knowing what he should say.

"The truth is, my father grew to fear the ocean," Nathaniel began again. "Not in the way we spoke of, for his was a terror that twisted his soul and robbed him of any good he could do."

Jack felt a tug on his oar as a large wave rolled under them.

"You see, my mother was lost at sea when I was just a babe," Nathaniel explained. "'Twas in the month of November. She had gone out with her brother on his sloop, and they lost their way home in a fog. My father took his dory out to find her, but he was too late. They never found her body. I wear this button on my cap as a keepsake. It came from her sewing basket."

He tilted his head forward, and as he did, Jack could see a twinkle of moonlight bouncing off the little brass anchor button.

"Ten years later almost to the day, my father and I were up in the lantern room," Nathaniel continued. "I was

eleven years old at the time. We were watching a storm that came wheeling up the coast when we spotted a sloop leaning into the shoal. The fog was creeping in all around her.

"My father ordered me to ring the fog bell while he took the dory out to try to rescue any survivors. But the gales were too strong, and by the time he fought his way past the breakers, 'twas too late. They had all perished. Among the five dead was a woman.

"I suppose 'twas on account of my father's finding that woman's body, and it being in the month of November, and his arriving too late once again…all those things played on his mind. For afterward he had terrible nightmares, nightmares that he woke from screaming. From then on, he had such a powerful fear of the sea that he wouldn't set foot in a boat. Do you take my meaning, Jack?"

"Uh, I think so," Jack answered as he looked out over the inky black waves. "You mean he didn't want to take the dory out on the water?"

"Didn't and wouldn't," Nathaniel cried. "And what is a keeper's job but to safeguard those who founder along his shores? To take his skiff out and rescue those who are in need? My father was only half a keeper after that. He kept the light and rang the bell, but he wouldn't venture out to save those unfortunate enough to wreck in our cove. And for those that perished, half a keeper was as bad as no keeper at all."

Jack looked back at the glowing lighthouse and wondered what it must have been like to wreck in the cove.

"The closest he came to a ship after that were the models he made," Nathaniel continued. "For all his fear of the sea, 'twas a strange thing that grabbed hold of his heart then. The making of model ships! I'd watch him night after night, carving in front of the fire. He had a special knife he used. It had a handle made of whalebone, with a sea horse on one side and on the other a compass rose.

"With each new ship he made," Nathaniel said, shaking his head, "I think he imagined himself taking her out. Guiding her past the breakwater, out to the open sea. But that was all in his mind. Those ships sailed no further than the fireplace mantel, and they came one after the other until I could not bear the sight of them. My father turned into a coward then, Jack, and 'twas my shame to be his son."

Jack sat dumbfounded. He had never imagined having a father who could be a failure! It seemed the exact opposite of his own problem. For while Nathaniel's father had lost his nerve and failed, his own father never made mistakes.

"All that winter I prayed that he'd get his nerve back,"

Nathaniel continued. "And I've never told another, not even Tom. At first I told myself 'twas out of fear of my father's losing his post, but 'twas more than that, for Tom wouldn't have told. I suppose I was afeard of losing my friend, losing his respect. But I'm telling you now, Jack. Because I've forgiven my father."

"How?" Jack asked. "How could you forget what he'd done?"

Nathaniel looked him in the eye. "I didn't say forget, I said forgive. And forgiveness is a funny thing, Jack. You may think you're doing it for someone else, but you come to find that 'tis your own heart that's been weighted down by an anger only *you* can let go of."

Jack felt a heaviness in his own chest then as he thought of his father and the anger he felt toward him lately.

"My father was a good man who did a bad thing," Nathaniel continued. "But in the end, the thing they accused him of was far worse. And that's why I need your help."

"Me?" Jack asked, surprised. "What can I do to help?"

"You can help me to clear my father's name and the accusations that were made."

"What?" Jack whispered as a fish rippled the water beside his oar. "What did they accuse him of?"

Nathaniel's face darkened. The sea suddenly came up

from behind them, lifting the boat and setting it roughly back down. Jack was still catching his breath when he heard Nathaniel's voice rise above the sound of an approaching wave.

"They accused him of a cowardliness so shameful his name has been blackened these hundred years past."

Nathaniel fell silent as Jack sat waiting.

"What was it, Nathaniel?" he finally asked. "What did they accuse him of that was so bad?"

Nathaniel fixed his eyes on Jack's. "They said it was on account of him that his son died. They said that Keeper Samuel Witherspoon was too much of a coward to try to rescue his own son."

Jack leaned back in the boat, trying to take it all in.

"What are you saying, Nathaniel?" he whispered. "That your father let you—"

"No!" Nathaniel cried, his voice rising over the crashing waves. "No, he tried to save me, Jack. You must believe me! He died trying to save me! And that's what I need to prove. He got his courage back, and I need you to help me prove it."

Another strong wave rocked the boat and sent Jack sliding to his left. When he righted himself, he noticed that Nathaniel hadn't budged.

"Will you help me, Jack?" Nathaniel asked, his blue eyes pleading now.

"I'll do whatever I can," Jack replied. "But I don't know where to begin. I don't know what I—"

"Just promise me, Jack. Promise to help."

"Okay, I promise," Jack whispered.

Nathaniel smiled. "You've got a curious mind, Jack, and a strong imagination. You'll find a way. It may take you a while, but you'll find a way." He turned to look back at the shore.

Jack turned to look with him. Their eyes followed the tower's roving beam, over the water and onto the beach. And although Jack Carlton didn't have the slightest idea of how he was going to keep his promise to Nathaniel Witherspoon, he knew he would have to try.

"What do you say we take her in, mate?" Nathaniel called.

"Right, mate," Jack replied with a grin.

And that's exactly what they did. With one sailor at the oars and the other at the stern, the little blue dory made its way smoothly under the stars, through the breakwater, and onto the stony beach of Lizard Light.

CHAPTER TWENTY-FOUR

When Jack awoke the next morning, the first thing he did was to feel the blisters on the palms of his hands. He smiled as he looked down at his reddened skin. Those blisters were proof of his courage and proof that he could do something right. He could handle a boat. He could be a good sailor. But Jack knew that he couldn't share this proof with just anyone. In fact, there was only one special someone that he dared confide in, and that was his lizard.

It wasn't until he went to look in the terrarium that Jack realized Ned was missing. As he played back the events of the night in his mind, Jack realized that he had never put Ned back into the terrarium! Worse still, he had left his bedroom door open!

Jack threw off the bed sheets and lifted his pillow. He shook out his quilt and crawled under his bed. He threw everything his mother had so neatly placed in his closet out onto the rug. All the while, he called Ned's name, begging him to come out. But after searching for more than an hour, Jack still found no sign of him.

Jack knew that as loyal a lizard as Ned was, he was also an adventurous one. And that meant he could be anywhere! What if he had followed Jack and Nathaniel outside? What if he was wandering alone on the beach right now? What if a wave had carried him off? Or a gull had swooped down and gobbled him up for a meal?

Not surprisingly, Jack's father scolded him at breakfast. "Ned deserves better than that. If you had kept him in the terrarium, where he belongs, you wouldn't have this problem now."

Jack gritted his teeth and kicked the leg of the table with his sneaker. He bet his dad was glad to have some new material for his lectures.

"Don't worry, we'll find him," his mother said consolingly. "He has to be somewhere in this house. How far could he have gotten?"

You don't want to know, Jack thought miserably. You don't want to know.

After breakfast, Mr. Carlton left for work and Mrs. Carlton and Franny helped Jack search. Mrs. Carlton got down on her hands and knees in front of the stove and waved a piece of lettuce as she called, "Ned! Here, Ned! Come on, fella."

Franny, meanwhile, sprinkled a trail of her candy pills all through the living room and into the dining room. Her hope was to lure the lizard with her powerful medicine. As much as Jack appreciated their efforts, he couldn't stop the tears that were welling in his eyes. For if Ned had gotten outside, what were his chances of coming back in?

Jack spent the rest of the morning searching the house

and then headed outside. But as he walked along the beach, any hopes of finding Ned were soon dashed. Jack could see that there were just too many places for the lizard to lose his way. There were too many rocks for him to crawl under. There was too much beach for him to get lost on and too much surf to carry him off. "Ned, Ned, please come back, buddy," Jack continued to call.

After lunch, his mother interrupted the search to remind Jack to do his math work sheets before his father came home. Jack quickly raced through his page of problems so he could get back to looking. But hours later, after searching inside and out, there was still no sign of Ned.

Jack's face was so forlorn at supper that Mr. Carlton offered to move the refrigerator away from the wall so they could have a look behind it. Jack was surprised and relieved that he was willing to help. It felt like old times, before he and his father had become so distant.

Mr. Carlton reached in behind the refrigerator to grab hold and pushed it out from the wall.

"No, he's not back here," he called, looking behind the refrigerator. When Mrs. Carlton heard her husband say, "All right, let's get this baby back," she decided to help. She started to push, and Jack did, too. Then they heard Mr. Carlton's sudden cry. They had pinned his arm against the wall!

Everyone piled into the car, and Mrs. Carlton drove to

an emergency room, which was three towns over. Mr. Carlton insisted that when he had said, "Let's get this baby back," he was talking to himself. He hadn't expected anyone else to push!

In the back seat, Jack sat with his head in his hands, staring out the window. No one was blaming him, but they didn't have to. He knew that if he hadn't lost Ned, his father wouldn't have had to move the refrigerator in the first place.

When they arrived at the hospital, Jack trailed inside after everyone else. After taking X rays, a doctor told Mr. Carlton that he had a bad sprain and would need to wear his arm in a sling for a week or more.

"Well, this is a great way for the new principal to look as he begins the year," Mr. Carlton grumbled as he got into the passenger's seat with his sling. No one spoke for the entire ride home.

After they returned to the cottage, Franny got down on all fours and crawled through the living room, gobbling up her pills as she went.

"And just what are you doing?" Mrs. Carlton demanded.

"Someone's got to eat the medicine if Ned won't," Franny mumbled, her mouth full of candy pills.

"Spit those out right now, young lady," Mrs. Carlton insisted. "You are not a lizard. You are a girl. And girls do not eat off the floor." None of this made Jack feel any better.

Later that night, he lay awake in his bed, watching as the light from the tower circled his room. When it shone on the empty terrarium, he felt a lump in his throat. He wiped away a tear.

In all his hurry to be good at something and to prove himself, he had let down his pet. He had failed again. His father was right, Jack thought. Ned did deserve a better owner.

With his flashlight switched on and a pile of lettuce leaves lying on his bed, Jack sat up to wait. This time he wasn't waiting for one friend, but two. He opened a book on shell collecting. He read about periwinkles and how they have lots of tiny teeth on their tongues, which they use to eat algae.

Jack stuck out his tongue as far as he could. Then he turned the page and looked at a picture of a long blue mussel shell. The words under the illustration said that the mussel inside had probably been eaten by a dog whelk. Jack held his flashlight over the picture and continued to read. "Dog whelks like to drill a hole in the mussel shell and then suck out the soft part."

When he finally fell asleep later that night, Jack dreamt that Ned had crawled into a mussel shell and a giant dog whelk was sucking him out!

CHAPTER
TWENTY-FIVE

Jack spent the next three days searching for Ned, looking for mussel shells and dog whelk holes, and rushing through his math work sheet problems. Each day, Jack continued to search along the beach for Ned while gathering new shells for his collection.

The thought that Ned could be gone forever was so depressing that Jack tried to get his mind onto something else. He thought about starting school on the following Monday, but that made him feel even worse.

He worried about being the new kid in school, and being the principal's son only made things harder. Who would want to talk to him? Who would want to be his friend?

The only bright spot in his future was the news that his Uncle Quentin would be arriving on that Thursday. And when his mother went to use the phone on Thursday morning and discovered that the line was once again dead, Jack panicked.

"What if Uncle Quentin gets lost and can't find us?" Jack asked anxiously. "What if he's trying to call?"

"Your uncle's middle name could be Marco Polo," Mrs. Carlton told him. "Why, when we were growing up, I remember his room was always full of maps. He was the only kid I knew who got maps in his stocking at Christmas! You don't ever have to worry about Uncle Quentin getting lost."

Jack knew his mother was right. His uncle did have a great sense of direction. He knew all about maps and boats and things that Jack's father knew nothing about, things that Jack was secretly learning.

Uncle Quentin had a special knife with a little sail-boat etched on the handle. Jack loved to look at that knife. He wondered if his uncle would let him use it to cut some rope so that he could show him the knots he'd learned to tie. But more than anything, Jack couldn't wait to go out in his uncle's boat and show him what a good sailor he could be.

The morning of Uncle Quentin's arrival, Jack's father decided that he had better stay home with his "broken wing," as he called his sprained arm.

"I'm more of an inlander at heart, anyway," Mr. Carlton joked.

While Jack and Franny watched at the window for Uncle Quentin's car, Mr. Carlton decided to check Jack's math work sheets. He had been so busy with his new job that he hadn't corrected them in days.

Jack decided that it might be a good time to make himself scarce. He had rushed through so many of the problems on the work sheets that he knew most of them were wrong and many were just unfinished. He was silently tiptoeing toward the back door when he heard his father growl, "Jack! Get in here right now!"

Jack slunk into the dining room.

"What is the meaning of this?" Mr. Carlton demanded, waving the work sheets in the air with his good arm. "Do you call this effort? What do you have to say for yourself?"

Jack shrugged and lowered his eyes to the floor. "I wasn't in the mood," he said glumly.

As soon as he said it, Jack realized that it was the wrong thing to say.

CHAPTER TWENTY-SIX

What Jack had meant was that he was too worried about Ned to concentrate and that he was too sad to do math. But it had come out sounding fresh. It had come out sounding all wrong!

"Well, then I guess you won't be in the mood to go sailing with Uncle Quentin," his father retorted. "You can stay home with me and redo all of these pages. And I'm telling you right now, you'd better get into the mood to concentrate and give this your complete attention, or you're going to be sorry!"

Jack was at the dining room table, working on his problems, when he heard a car on the graveled driveway. He looked out the window to see Uncle Quentin's Jeep pulling a long black-and-white sailboat.

After getting permission to leave the table, he raced out the front door past his parents. Uncle Quentin laughed to see Jack and Franny tripping over each other to get to him. Their uncle was a big man with a full dark beard and a ready smile. He reached out to give Jack a bear hug and then picked up Franny in his arms. Jack fought back his tears when he heard his uncle ask, "Is everyone ready for a sail?"

Mr. Carlton quickly explained that he and Jack would be

staying home. Jack looked at Uncle Quentin's boat, with its new paint and folded white sails, and he felt his mouth quivering with disappointment. He quickly lowered his eyes to the ground.

Uncle Quentin tried to persuade his brother-in-law to change his mind and let Jack go, but Mr. Carlton stood firmly shaking his head.

"Jack's got to learn responsibility," he said. "He's got to own up to his mistakes and take the consequences."

"Aren't you being a little hard on the boy?" Uncle Quentin said gently, putting his hand on Jack's shoulder. "Why don't you give him a break?"

"Jack has gotten off to a bit of a bad start since we moved here, Quentin," Mr. Carlton explained. "And he has to work hard now at turning that around. I'm sorry he'll miss the boat ride, but he's just going to have to learn the hard way."

Fifteen minutes later, Jack was back sitting at the table, chewing on the end of his pencil. He could hear everyone talking excitedly as they stood outside the cottage to have their picture taken.

"Isn't the wind too strong for you to be going out?" he heard his father ask.

"That's what sailboats like," Uncle Quentin quipped. "Wind is our friend."

"But it's so strong today," Mr. Carlton worried. "And, Jen, where's your life jacket?"

"Will you stop?" Mrs. Carlton groaned. "Franny's got one on, and I'm bringing mine along. I'll put it on if I need it. And you're forgetting that we have a sailor in the family. My big brother will save me if I need him. Won't you, Quentin?"

They all laughed, and then their voices faded as they headed for the beach. With a frown, Jack bent his head back over his paper. He did three more problems and looked out the dining room window. He could see his uncle lifting Franny into the sailboat. Her bright orange life jacket matched the sparkly orange Band-Aids she had put all over her legs that morning. Jack watched his mother get into the boat next to her. The wind was blowing so hard it blew off her hat. Mr. Carlton caught it before it went into the water, and everyone waved and clapped their hands. Uncle Quentin stood by the mast and adjusted the rigging.

Jack ground his pencil point into his paper as he looked away. He spent the next ten minutes trying to concentrate on the problems in front of him, but it was impossible to think. He had never hated math so much. And he had never hated his father more than he did at that moment.

All he cares about are these stupid problems, with these stupid numbers, Jack thought.

"I hate them! I hate them and I hate you!" he cried out as he jammed his broken pencil point down through the numbers, ripping the paper as he did.

When his fury subsided, Jack looked down, horrified to see the damage he had done. The paper was so badly shredded he couldn't read any of the problems! What would his father say when he saw it? And what excuse could he give?

Once again he had messed up. He was never going to "turn things around." He was always going to be a failure in his father's eyes. And he knew that along with his father's disappointment would come a punishment. Jack decided that the only way out was to destroy the evidence. He couldn't say the dog ate the work sheet, because they had no dog. He couldn't say the baby chewed it, because they had no baby. Jack began to feel deprived. Why couldn't they have dogs or babies in their family the way other people did? Why did his life have to be so hard?

Jack sat with his head in his hands. He knew that his father would be back inside any minute and would discover what he had done. There was nothing he could do but wait for the storm to hit.

As he waited, Jack stared absentmindedly across the room. His eye caught sight of a bright pink dot on the rug. There were four more dots that followed it, forming a line. Jack realized that they were one of Franny's medicine trails. He was about to get up to retrieve a pill to help his depressed condition when he spotted one of Franny's orange Band-Aids beside the hutch cabinet. The bright orange of the Band-Aid reminded Jack of Franny's orange life jacket, and he frowned.

If only he could have been wearing one of those life jackets right now. If only he could have been out on the boat. He sat staring at the Band-Aid, feeling worse and worse. He watched as it shuffled over to the medicine trail and stopped at the first pink pill.

Jack's left eyebrow shot up when he realized what he had just seen. He had just seen a walking Band-Aid!

Jack held his breath as he silently slipped off his chair and started for the other side of the room. He stopped suddenly as the Band-Aid moved on to another pill. Getting down on his knees, Jack crawled over to the medicine trail and pressed his cheek to the rug. Under the Band-Aid he could see four little legs. Four little green legs!

"Ned!" Jack cried, scooping up the Band-Aided lizard. He gently pulled the sticky orange coating off Ned's back, and the grateful lizard happily flicked his tongue.

"Oh, Ned! I'm so glad I found you," Jack exclaimed as he carried him back to the table. "I'm never going to leave you like that again. I promise I won't."

Jack sat down in his chair and placed Ned beside his work sheet. Ned took one look at the torn paper and began to nibble it.

"Ned, you really are a genius!" Jack cried. "This is perfect. Now I can tell Dad that my lizard ate my homework! Keep chewing, boy, keep chewing. Oh, Ned, this is the happiest day of my life!"

Just at that moment, Jack heard his father's shout. But it wasn't an angry shout. It was a scared shout.

Jack jumped from his seat so fast the chair fell over. He raced to the window to see his father holding his hand to his head and screaming as he looked out over the sea. Jack tried to find his uncle's boat, but couldn't. Something was wrong. Something was terribly wrong.

Jack darted from the window and rushed to the front door. He flew out of the house and ran down the beach toward his father. Jack scanned the water for the sailboat, but he still couldn't find it.

"Where are they, Dad?" he shouted.

"Out there," his father cried, pointing past the breakers to the capsized sailboat, which was floating on its side. "The mast snapped in the wind, and the whole thing tipped right over!"

Jack could see his uncle in the water, holding on to the rigging as he tried to reach for Franny. Her head was bobbing above her life jacket. She seemed to be drifting away from him. Jack searched all around the boat for his mother. But there was no sign of her.

"Mom!" he screamed. "Where is she?"

"She's gone under, Jack!" his father cried. "She's gone under!"

CHAPTER
TWENTY-SEVEN

"We've got to do something!" Mr. Carlton shouted, pacing back and forth over the sand. "Jack, quick—run in the house and call the police. The number is on the board. Tell them to send the Coast Guard. Tell them to hurry!"

"But, Dad, the phone's not working," Jack reminded him. "Besides, it would take them too long to get here."

"What are we going to do?" Mr. Carlton asked anxiously. "I should never have let them go in this wind. I should have talked Quentin out of it."

Jack suddenly thought of Nathaniel's mother and how she too had gone out on her brother's boat. Only she had never come back!

"The dory!" Jack cried. "We can take out the dory."

"The what?"

"The dory, the boat in the boathouse," Jack shouted as he began to run down the beach.

"But, but, I don't know anything about boats..." Mr. Carlton was scrambling behind him.

"That's okay, I do," Jack cried over the wind.

His father gave him a puzzled look, but there was no time to explain. They were almost to the boathouse when Jack saw the lock. His heart sank at the sight of it, but as he got closer, he saw a sparkle of light bouncing off the small brass key that was still inside it.

"He left the key in!" Jack gasped.

"Who? Wha-wha-what are you talking about?" Mr. Carlton stammered, coming up behind him.

"Never mind," Jack said. "Let's just get it open." He turned the key and opened the lock. With his one good arm, Mr. Carlton helped Jack pull the door back with such force that it slammed against the little building. Jack threw the oars into the dory and then pulled a life preserver and rope from the wall. Mr. Carlton grabbed a life jacket from a nail and threw it over one shoulder. Jack did the same.

"Where do you think you're going?" Mr. Carlton said, seeing Jack's life jacket.

"With you," Jack said. "You can't manage alone with that sling. And what if you had another heart attack?"

"I feel as if I could have one right now," Mr. Carlton mumbled as they dragged the dory over the beach and down to the surf line. Jack scanned the water. The wind had picked up, and a gray mist was rolling in. The downed sailboat was drifting farther out in the heavy gusts. He could see heads bobbing, but he could no longer make them out.

"I can row, Dad," Jack told him. "I can do it."

"You? What do you know about rowing a boat?" his father scoffed as he went to push the dory into the surf.

"No, Dad, wait." Jack stopped him as he pulled on the gunwales. "You've got to position your oarlocks and get your oars in place before you get her in the water. We're going to have to fight this westerly to get past the breakers."

Mr. Carlton stood speechless as Jack hurried to position the oars. "Where did you learn all that?" he asked. Luckily, he was too distracted to wait for an answer.

"We've got to get out there," Jack screamed over the wind. "You take the stern, Dad, and I'll row. Get in."

Mr. Carlton was in such a state of panic and so dumbstruck by Jack's confident handling of the boat that he did as he was told. Jack waited for the tide to begin to pull back and then gave the boat a shove. But the water wasn't deep enough, and the dory didn't budge.

Jack felt his confidence slipping away as he sensed his father's eyes on him. His stomach tightened into a knot. His arms began to go limp, and his knees began to buckle.

I can't do it! he suddenly thought. What made me ever think I could?

But then he heard his father cry out to his mother as he jumped out of the boat. "Jen, we're coming! Try to hang on!"

His father's heartrending plea shook Jack out of his fearful stupor. I have to do it right, I will do it right, he told himself as his father leaned against the other side of the dory. Together they gave the boat another shove and quickly jumped in.

Jack soon learned what Nathaniel had meant about "fighting the wind," for the gusts were so strong that it took all his strength to keep the oars moving. As he dragged them through the choppy sea, Jack imagined Nathaniel's voice calling to him: "Pull, pull!"

But the surf was so strong and the wind so fierce that they were making little headway. Jack began to doubt they'd ever reach the sailboat.

When a giant wave lifted them into the air, Jack felt his stomach drop. They rose higher and higher, as if on some terrifying roller-coaster ride. Jack squeezed his eyes shut tight. Suddenly, without warning, the wave broke and came crashing down.

"Aagh!" he and his father screamed together. The boat hit the water with such force that they were both nearly thrown overboard. Jack tried hard to regain his composure and to get his concentration back on the rowing. But his teeth were chattering so loudly they rattled his thinking. Gasping to catch his breath, he half expected to hear his father yell for him to change seats. He expected to

hear how he was doing it all wrong. But when their eyes did meet, Jack saw only fear in his father's eyes.

"Are you all right?" Mr. Carlton called from the stern.

Jack tried hard not to cry. "Yeah, Dad, I'm okay," he yelled back into the wind.

"You're doing great, son," his father encouraged him. And with those few words, Jack felt his knees growing steady and his nerve returning. He dipped the oars back into the water and pulled as hard as he could. He pulled until the dory fought through the wind and pushed through the waves. He pulled until the blisters on his palms broke and his arms felt as if they were being wrenched from their sockets. He pulled and he pulled, and he didn't stop pulling until he finally heard the one voice that made it all worth it.

"Jack!" he heard his mother call. "Oh, thank God, Jack!"

CHAPTER TWENTY-EIGHT

Luckily, no one had been hurt too badly in the accident, except Uncle Quentin, who had a cut on his forehead and a sprained ankle. Franny gave him a sparkly orange Band-Aid for each. Mrs. Carlton declared that she would never again get into a boat without first putting on a life jacket. She and Franny had been badly shaken up by the misadventure, but they quickly recovered.

Ned had stayed put through the whole thing. Jack found his lizard asleep under the work sheet on the dining room table. Ned hadn't eaten much of the paper, but in all the excitement Mr. Carlton forgot about the math problems and never even asked to see them.

The day after the accident, Mrs. Carlton made "hero sandwiches" for a special celebration dinner and baked a cake decorated with Life Savers. To thank Jack for saving his life, Uncle Quentin gave him his special knife, the one with the sailboat carved on it. Franny gave him her entire supply of candy medicine. Jack felt as if it were his birthday and Christmas all rolled into one.

But as good as all of these things were, the very best thing was what had happened between Jack and his father in the blue dory, out on that choppy sea. They had done something important together. They had worked as a team. It had brought them together.

The night of the accident, as Ned looked on from his terrarium, two figures sat on the edge of Jack's bed. And as the glow from the tower swept across the old quilt and the lull of the waves echoed from the open window, Jack leaned back against his pillow.

"You made me very proud today," Mr. Carlton told him. "Proud and ashamed. Ashamed that I hadn't seen that the very things I'd been hoping to teach you were there all along. Sometimes even grownups mess up, Jack. And sometimes we need to learn lessons, too."

Jack didn't know what to say. He had never heard his father admit to messing up before.

"We moved to Minty because I made some mistakes back in Iowa. Some mistakes in my job," his father said.

Jack was flabbergasted! He had never imagined his father failing at something, especially something as big as his job.

"But—but—you're always talking about standing out and doing things so perfectly," Jack sputtered.

"I guess that's a problem I have," Mr. Carlton sighed. "You see, Jack, I was expecting too much from my teachers, just like I expected too much from you. And it wasn't because I was perfect, but just the opposite. I was afraid I wasn't good enough. A good enough principal or a good enough father. I know I haven't been the best father these last few weeks. I've made mistakes, and I'm sorry."

Jack bit his lower lip. He felt all the anger he had pressed down for so long bubbling up to the top now. All the slights and the misunderstandings had piled up on top of each other. And it was hard to just forget them. His father sat waiting. Neither of them spoke.

Embarrassed, Jack lowered his eyes and fumbled nervously with the book in his hands. He traced his finger over the little gold anchor on the leather spine, and he was suddenly reminded of another boy and another father. Samuel Witherspoon had made mistakes, too, big ones. But his son had forgiven him. And then Nathaniel's words came back to him: "Forgiveness is a funny thing, Jack. You may think you're doing it for someone else, but you come to find that 'tis your heart that's been weighted down by an anger only you can let go of."

Jack looked up into his father's dark eyes. He could smell the familiar minty scent of his aftershave. He could see the worry lines forming on his forehead.

"When I told you this move to Maine could be a fresh start, I meant a fresh start for me as well as for you," his father whispered.

"I think it has been, Dad," Jack said, feeling a heaviness lift from his chest. "I think it has."

They sat up talking for a long time. Then Jack showed his father the different knots he had tied on his rope. Together the two of them tried the fisherman's bend as they pored over the instructions from Jack's book. When his father asked about his shell collection, Jack showed him a mussel shell and explained about the dog whelks sucking out the meat. He told him about periwinkles' tongues. The two were having so much fun together, Jack forgot all about waiting up for Nathaniel.

But Ned didn't forget. The little lizard had taken a special liking to the boy who stepped out of the light. Later that night, while Jack slept soundly, tucked under his covers, it was Ned who waited and watched for the keeper's son. But he never did come, not that night, or the next, or the one after that.

It wasn't until a few nights later that Jack finally did remember to wait up for Nathaniel. But he worried that his secret friend had been hurt by Jack's forgetting about him and that maybe he wouldn't come again. Just as he feared, the young ghost didn't make an appearance. Jack thought about his promise to Nathaniel, to help clear his father's name. He still had no ideas about how he could accomplish such a feat. He wondered if Nathaniel knew that and if maybe that was the reason he'd stopped coming. But as sorry as Jack was about not keeping his promise, he had little time to think about it. He was about to start his very first day as the principal's son at Minty Elementary School.

CHAPTER
TWENTY-NINE

When you are a new student in a school with only seventy-seven students in it, you tend to stick out. It's as if you had two heads. And when your father happens to be the school's new principal, it's as if you had twenty-two heads!

Jack hung his one and only head down for the car ride to his first day at Minty Elementary School the following week. He knew what to expect. He expected the worst. What he didn't know was that if you are a new student in a little school that has sand in the cracks of its old wooden floors and clam shells lining its walks, and you happen to get your picture on the front page of the local newspaper for a daring rescue by boat, you tend to stick out as well. You stick out just like a movie star!

All of Jack's worries about being ignored because he was the new kid in school or snubbed because he was the principal's son were over the minute he walked through Minty Elementary's big oak doors. Everyone wanted to meet the boy who was strong enough to row in a choppy sea, and smart enough to tie a life preserver to his dory with a bowline knot and then throw it to his drowning mother. Everyone wanted to shake his hand.

So many good things were happening all at once that Jack hardly had time to catch his breath. The first week of school was a whirlwind of activity as he settled in, meeting his new classmates and teachers. When a boy in Jack's class named Philip Knox told Jack about the rocks he collected, Jack told him all about Denton's collection, and the two talked rocks all through lunch.

It was a tradition at Minty Elementary that the fifth-grade class begin each school year with a trip to the local Minty Museum. Jack thought this was an excellent tradition, since it meant getting out of class and being able to walk the three blocks to the museum with his new friend, Philip.

It was also a tradition that the principal accompany the fifth graders on their field trip. Jack was surprised to find that he was glad his father was coming along. He supposed it had something to do with the fresh start they each had made.

Once they were inside the little museum, Miss Cook, the curator, explained that most of the exhibits were about the history of Minty. Mrs. Flannery, Jack's teacher, told her students, "See if you can discover some history about your families or where you live, and record it in your notebooks."

There were pictures of the old post office and the general store. But an exhibit on the history of the fishing industry in Minty attracted the biggest crowd.

When Philip left Jack's side to take notes along with the others, Jack's shoulders slumped. Everyone seemed to have found something to write about—everyone but him. He looked for his father, but Mr. Carlton was busy talking to Miss Cook.

"Jack, you might want to look at this exhibit," Mrs. Flannery said, pointing to a glass showcase.

Jack walked over to the case and looked inside. The first thing he saw was an old black-and-white photograph of a lighthouse. Beside the photograph was a ship in a bottle. The inscription under the old photo read LIZARD LIGHT 1850. Jack recognized the tower at once, but the walkway looked different. It had a roof.

Jack quickly opened his notebook and took a pencil out of his backpack. Then he turned his attention to the short written history beside the picture.

"Lizard Light was erected in the year 1838. It was known for its bright, dependable light and the ring of its fog bell. Its first keeper was Samuel Witherspoon."

"Samuel Witherspoon!" Jack whispered the name aloud. And his eyes grew big as sand dollars as he looked back at the ship in the bottle.

That must be one of his ships! Jack thought. One of the ones he made after he found that dead woman! Then Jack noticed the skull sitting beside the bottle.

"Old Pete!" he whispered, leaning closer to the case.

His eyes darted back to the history printed beside the photograph, and he felt his heart stop as he read the next paragraph.

"But it was the keeper's young son, twelve-year-old Nathaniel, who displayed untold courage in attempting to rescue the survivors of a whaler, the *Merlin*, that had gone down in the storm of 1851. It was one of the bravest rescues recorded in Minty's history—and, sadly, the most tragic."

Jack pressed his hand against the glass display case as he continued to read.

For it was not the keeper, Samuel Witherspoon, but his son, Nathaniel, who set out in a dory on that storm-tossed sea. And it was young Nathaniel who rescued the three lone sailors who survived. Sadly, on the return to shore, tragedy struck once more, as the little dory capsized in the rough surf and Nathaniel was drowned. Although his body was never found, the bravery of this young boy was not forgotten. For the three survivors of the shipwreck lived to tell of his heroic deed.

But the mystery remains. Why hadn't Keeper Witherspoon gone out himself? Word spread that he had lost his nerve and could not bring himself to brave the storm. But no one will ever know, for when the survivors did make it to shore, they found the light-house empty—as well as Neversink Cottage, which sat beside it. Both dories were missing from the boathouse.

Some believe that the keeper must have taken his boat out to try and get to the sinking *Merlin*. When he failed in his attempt and drowned, they say his young son followed him. But if that was the case, why did the survivors swear that it was only Nathaniel's dory they saw coming out of the fog? And why did they further swear that as the young boy helped to pull them from the downed ship, they could hear the fog bell ringing from shore? If Keeper Witherspoon had gone out first and drowned, who was ringing the bell?

It is a mystery that no one has ever solved, for Samuel Witherspoon disappeared without a trace, never to be heard from again. And while the keeper's position in Minty's history remains a mystery, the bravery and courage of his son, Nathaniel, live on.

"Oh, Nathaniel!" Jack choked down a sob. "Oh, mate!"

CHAPTER
THIRTY

"What's the matter with you?" Philip whispered in Jack's ear. "You look as if you've just seen a ghost."

"I have," Jack mumbled. "I have."

"Come on," Philip said, grabbing Jack's arm. "Stop hanging around here. You're missing the best part. Come see the wreck in the next room."

Jack was in such a daze that he hardly noticed as Philip led him through a doorway into a large, brightly lit room. He was still reeling from the discovery of Nathaniel's heroic death, reeling from the knowledge that Nathaniel had lost his life because of his father's cowardice. But that wasn't what Nathaniel had told him. He said his father had tried to save him—but how? And how could Jack prove it?

As he blinked back the tears that were filling his eyes, Jack looked up to see his own father smiling at him from across the room. Jack tried to smile back, but couldn't. He wanted desperately to go back to the showcase and read about Nathaniel again. He wanted to read how courageous Nathaniel had been to save those three sailors on the *Merlin*. But he found himself boxed in as all ten of his classmates gathered to see the large exhibit in the center of the room.

Jack hardly took notice of the wooden hulk of a ship's bow that was on display within blue velvet ropes. As if in a dream, he heard the curator, Miss Cook, announce: "We are so excited that the remains of this old whaling ship have been given to the Minty Museum. I would ask you all to please not touch the wood or lean too far over the rope. The bow is displayed on a tilt so that you can look inside. Since the wreck has been lying under the ocean for more than a hundred years, there are some rotted planks, and shipworms have taken their toll. What you see before you is a piece of history. And it is our job here at the museum to preserve it.

"Unfortunately, shipwrecks have played a big part in Minty's history. The wreck you are looking at was recovered from the waters off Lizard Light just this past spring. The name of the ship was the *Merlin*, and it sank in a storm in the year 1851. If you'll move on into the next room, we do have a display that tells about the courageous boy who lost his life to..." Miss Cook's words blurred into the background as a wave of shock washed over Jack.

He gripped the velvet rope in his hands to steady himself as he realized what he was looking at. He was looking at the wreck of the whaler, the *Merlin*, that had cost his friend his life!

Suddenly, Jack felt an uncontrollable urge to touch the

wreck, to touch this fateful link to Nathaniel. The urge grew so strong that before he could stop himself he leaned over the velvet rope and put his hand out to touch the wood. But he leaned so far that he lost his balance and pitched headfirst into the ship!

Jack could hear Miss Cook's scream and his father's voice yelling, "No, Jack!" as he went over. He could hear his classmates' stunned gasps and shouts as they pressed together at the rope.

Jack sat up as quickly as he could. Miss Cook, meanwhile, rushed under the rope and offered to help pull him out. He looked up to see his father's frowning face beside her.

Oh, no! Jack thought. I've done it again! I've let him down, and this time I've done it in a really big way, in front of the entire fifth grade!

He felt his face flush with embarrassment as a wave of snickers and whispers rippled through the room. But Jack's embarrassment soon turned to horror as he got to his feet and heard a loud *crack!*

Jack looked down to see his sneaker breaking through the rotted plank of wood he stood on! Miss Cook lurched forward to try to grab his T-shirt, but it was too late. The damage was done. His foot had gone all the way through the ship's floorboards, straight through the first deck!

Jack didn't have the courage to look at his father's face

this time. He knew what he would see. He knew that this latest episode was far worse than anything he had ever done in the past. He had gotten into trouble plenty of times, but he had never ruined a piece of history!

This is the worst day of my life, Jack thought miserably.

But as he lifted his sneaker from the hole, Jack spotted something below his foot. He leaned in for a closer look and was stunned to find that what he was looking at was a tiny sea horse.

"Jack!" his father exclaimed. "What are you doing? Get out of there right now, before you do any more damage!"

But before his father could stop him, Jack reached into the hole and pulled out an old rusted knife with a whale-bone handle. Etched on one side of the handle was a tiny sea horse. He quickly turned it over in his trembling hand and found a compass rose decorating the other side.

"His father's knife!" Jack whispered. "It's his father's knife!"

CHAPTER THIRTY-ONE

"Whose father?" Mr. Carlton asked as he helped to lift Jack over the wreck.

"Oh, my word!" Miss Cook exclaimed, reaching for the knife. "Look at that—the scrimshaw is still in perfect condition. Why, you've made an important discovery, young man. This must have belonged to one of the sailors on the *Merlin!*"

"No," Jack told her. "It belonged to Nathaniel's father. It belonged to Samuel Witherspoon."

"Samuel Witherspoon?" Mr. Carlton repeated. "What are you talking about?"

"He's talking about the original lighthouse keeper at Lizard Light," Miss Cook said. "But, Jack, what makes you say that?"

"He did just read the history of the light and the mystery of the lost keeper," Mrs. Flannery pointed out.

"And so is that why you imagine it was Keeper Witherspoon's knife?" Miss Cook asked.

"I don't imagine it. I *know* it!" Jack said vehemently. "This is the knife he used to carve that ship in the bottle you have in the case. I can't prove it. I just *know* it.

"And that means he did take his dory out! Not before Nathaniel, but after, to try and save him. He must have reached the *Merlin* before she went down. He was look-ing for Nathaniel. Don't you see? He must have drowned too, but before he did, he found his courage."

"He's always had an active imagination," Mr. Carlton said weakly.

"It's an unusual theory," murmured Miss Cook. "I'd be interested to hear more."

The next day, Jack's picture was in the *Minty Times* once again. He was standing beside Miss Cook, Mrs. Flannery, and his father on the steps of the Minty Museum. The grownups were all smiling. Jack was smil-ing, too, as he held the old rusted knife with the whale-bone handle. Under the photo the caption read BOY BREAKS THROUGH ONE PIECE OF HISTORY TO FIND AN-OTHER.

The story went on to describe Jack's accidental discov-ery and his "imaginative" theory for solving the mystery of Lizard Light. Miss Cook was quoted as saying, "No one has ever made such a speculation before, as far as I know." She went on to say, "Although we have no proof that the knife belonged to Samuel Witherspoon, it must be noted that we have no proof that it did not. And since Jack Carlton was the one who made this important discovery, this link to the past, I feel it is only fitting that we print his imaginative theory and display it in the showcase be-side the knife."

Jack's father bought a dozen copies of the paper. He had the picture and the story framed for his office. He also cut out a copy for the refrigerator. Jack took one copy for himself and one to send to Denton.

That night as Jack and Ned sat up reading in bed, Jack shone his flashlight on the newspaper story for Ned to see. But the little lizard seemed more interested in licking a chocolate chip cookie that was lying on the quilt. Jack had laid in a large supply of cookies, along with lettuce, for the wait.

"We'll stay up all night if we have to," he whispered, looking down at the newspaper. "Nathaniel *has* to come tonight. He has to see this. He has to know that his father's name is cleared."

Ned blinked in agreement and flicked his tongue at the cookie.

Together the two waited and waited, until they were the only ones left awake at Neversink Cottage. Even Huxley was dreaming in his bowl. As the beam from the tower poured in through the window, Jack held his flashlight over one open book and then another. He read aloud as Ned scurried across pictures of clamshells and sea stars and tripped lightly over schooners and sailboats.

But as Jack's voice grew weaker and his eyes began to close, Ned stopped scurrying and settled down to sleep atop an anchor at the bottom of a page.

Sometime later, a salty breeze blew across the quilt, rustling the pages of the book and waking the little lizard from his ocean dreams. He cocked his head to see Jack sleeping soundly, the flashlight still in his hand. Ned tilted his head back, listening. A seaweedy scent suddenly blew in through the open window, and he knew at once whose sandy footsteps were scratching across the floorboards toward the bed.

When the beam from the tower returned, Ned found himself looking up into the blue eyes of the keeper's son!

Nathaniel threw Ned a wink before leaning over to read the newspaper story in Jack's lap. Ned watched as the familiar face dimpled into a grin. Meanwhile, the tower's beam moved slowly across the quilt, and once again the room was thrown into darkness.

The little lizard blinked hard as he heard the sandy footsteps move away. And suddenly on the breeze came a whisper, a ghostly whisper, low and soft as a raven's wing.

"You kept your promise, just as I knew you would. Good-bye, mate. And thanks."

CHAPTER
THIRTY-TWO

Although Jack waited night after night, Nathaniel never did come to visit again. And over time, the ache of missing him lessened, just as the ache of missing Denton had lessened. It wasn't that Jack forgot them, it was just that it didn't hurt so much to think of them.

Jack's days were filled with school and his new friends. He roamed the beach with Franny and polished rocks with Philip and collected shells with his father.

Yet every once in a great while he would sit at the kitchen window and press his fingers over the little anchor carved there in the seat. It was then that Jack's thoughts returned to Nathaniel. And he began to think that maybe the young ghost was a friend he had just imagined, a friend who had never been real at all.

One foggy Saturday afternoon, weeks later, a knock came at the cottage door. It was a member of the Coast Guard, Will Howard, come to check on the tower. He wanted to know if any of the family would care for a tour of the lighthouse.

Jack looked up from his math work sheets at the dining room table. (Although he and his father had come to an understanding after their trip in the dory, they tended to fall back on old ways, as people will. Jack was still not the best student in math, and his father was still hoping he would be.) Jack tightened the grip on his pencil when he heard Mr. Howard's invitation. He had never told anyone of his secret visit up to the tower. He began to wonder if he really had gone up. Maybe he'd only imagined himself there. And maybe now was his chance to find out.

Jack anxiously followed his parents down the walkway and stepped through the tower's low, rounded doorway. His nose instantly picked up the scent of fresh paint and turpentine. He recognized the cool dampness coming off the tower's walls, or at least he thought he did. He stared at the bright white walls and dark blue trim everywhere. He struggled to remember those colors, but couldn't. Things looked different in the daylight.

"You're lucky today. On account of this fog coming in, the light is on," Mr. Howard said as the Carltons all gathered around the staircase.

"Is there an elevator?" Franny asked, looking up at all of the steps.

"Sorry, no elevators," Mr. Howard chuckled. "Just lots and lots of steps."

"How many?" Franny asked.

"I couldn't really say," Mr. Howard said, scratching his chin. "I don't think I ever really counted."

"One hundred and two," Jack said softly.

Mr. Carlton's eyebrows shot up. "And just how would you know that?" he asked.

"Just a guess." Jack shrugged.

"Sounds like a pretty good guess," Mr. Howard said. "We'd best start climbing if we're going to get to the top." Everyone followed behind him. Everyone but Jack.

He stood at the bottom step, wanting desperately to be alone, alone with his secret friend. The others had nearly reached the top when he began to climb.

Slowly, Jack made his way up to the first landing, then came to a sudden stop. For there before him, standing at the tower window, was the faint image of a boy. The boy was wiping the pane with a rag. Pushed back on his head was a worn white cap.

CHAPTER THIRTY-THREE

When the boy turned his head, Jack could see the ocean blue of his eyes and the special dimpled grin he knew so well. The image was so faint, Jack had to squint to see it. The ghost boy continued up the staircase.

"Wait!" Jack cried, running after him. "Nathaniel! I need to talk to you!" But the higher he climbed, the fainter the figure became. Suddenly, he disappeared altogether.

"Jack, hurry." Mr. Carlton's voice suddenly echoed down the stairs. "We can't take all of Mr. Howard's time. He does have a job to do. Come on up now, before he has to get back to work."

Jack climbed the stairs past the gallery door to the lantern room, all the while keeping an eye out for Nathaniel.

"I'd have thought you'd be the first one up here," Mr. Carlton said when Jack appeared at the top of the stairs.

Jack gave the modern light a quick look. Then as the grownups began talking, he walked past them over to the windows.

"Of course, when the tower first went up, they didn't have an automated light," Mr. Howard was saying.

"What did they burn to keep the old-time lamps going?" Mrs. Carlton asked.

"Whale oil," Jack murmured as he pressed his head to the windowpane. "About ten gallons a day." Everyone turned to look at him. "At least that's what I would guess," he quickly added.

"He's a darn good guesser," Mr. Howard said, shooting Jack a suspicious look.

"He has quite an imagination." Mr. Carlton smiled and shook his head.

Mr. Howard went on to explain how the lamps were kept, but Jack wasn't listening. He was too busy looking through the window at the pair of black wings that were suddenly fluttering before him!

As he pressed his head against the glass, Jack watched a ghostly black raven swoop down low and come to rest on the gallery's iron railing.

"Blackbeard!" Jack whispered under his breath.

"Jack, don't you want to come and see how the light works?" Mrs. Carlton called. But Jack couldn't tear his eyes away from the gallery walk below. For as the fog swirled around the tower's curve, he could see the faint image of a boy and a bird. Together they were looking out over the sea. Then slowly the boy turned and looked up at him. Jack squinted hard to see the sheepish grin on Nathaniel Witherspoon's face.

"Boo!" Franny yelled, coming up from behind. Jack spun around to face her.

"What are you looking at?" she demanded.

"Nothing," Jack whispered. "Nothing." He quickly turned back to the window and looked down, only to find that the walkway was empty. Jack squinted hard as he tried to see the young ghost and his pet raven, but they were nowhere to be found. He closed his eyes tight then and tried to call them back up, to imagine them once more, even if only in his mind. He tried to hear Blackbeard's croak, to listen for Nathaniel's whisper, but the only thing to reach his ears was Mr. Howard's deep voice saying, "Time to head down now, folks."

As he followed his family down the winding stairs, Jack began to wonder if he had ever really seen Nathaniel Witherspoon at all. Maybe his imagination was playing tricks on him once again. Maybe none of it had ever been real.

With a heavy heart, Jack followed his family out of the dark tower and into the bright autumn sunlight. He trailed behind his father and Mr. Howard, who were walking together to the boathouse.

"Oh, and I have the key," he heard his father say.

"Key? What key?" Mr. Howard asked.

"Why, the key to the boathouse. You must have left it in the lock the last time you were here," Mr. Carlton told him.

He went on to explain about the accident and how

he and Jack had used the dory in the rescue. Then he reached into his pocket and pulled out the little brass key.

"Well, this is news to me," Mr. Howard said, scratching his chin. "For as long as I've been checking on this light, there's been only one key to the boathouse lock. And it's right here on this ring." He held up his key chain and gave it a jangle.

"I'm the only one who opens this lock—once a month to check on the boathouse and see that everything is in order," he explained as he put his key in the lock and turned it.

"Well, I don't know about that. I'm just glad there was a key there when we needed it," Mr. Carlton said.

Jack stood watching as Mr. Howard pulled open the doors and looked in at the boat. "And she handled all right for you?" Mr. Howard asked.

"For my son," Mr. Carlton replied proudly. "He's the sailor in the family. He did all the rowing."

"Well, then I expect this button in here belongs to him," Mr. Howard said, reaching into the dory. He pulled out a button and handed it to Mr. Carlton.

Jack grinned as he remembered his pajama shirt button. His mother had been looking for it in the wash. In all the excitement he had forgotten how it had popped off as he rowed out with Nathaniel in the moonlight.

But Jack's face suddenly darkened. Had he really rowed out with Nathaniel? Or had he been alone, just imagining those twinkling blue eyes and that ghostly giggle? How would he ever know?

"Here you go, sailor," his father said, handing Jack the button.

At that moment, Jack Carlton knew—and would always know—the answer to his question. For the button his father had placed in his hand was neither red nor round as Jack had been expecting, but rather small, brass, and anchor-shaped.

Jack stared at the button in his palm.

"Looks as if we're going to have quite a sunset," he heard his father comment.

"Yep, it'll be a red sky tonight," Mr. Howard said as he locked the boathouse.

Jack took a deep breath of the cool salty air. The faint scent of decaying seaweed was on the breeze. "Red sky at night, sailor's delight," he whispered with a grin. And clutching the button in his hand, he looked back at the lighthouse.

"Thanks, mate," he whispered. "Thanks."

DEAR LEVI:
LETTERS FROM THE OVERLAND TRAIL

by Elvira Woodruff

It's 1851, and twelve-year-old Austin is setting off on a wagon train across the Overland Trail. Week by week, and letter by letter, Austin tells the story of his harrowing trip west, across miles of dusty roads and surging river waters—straight into Indian territory! It's a difficult journey and not all of his friends will survive. But it's a trip Austin's determined to make—for at the end lies the promise of a bright new life.

"Filled with hazardous escapades that keep the adrenaline pumping." —*Booklist*

"Presents a bounty of information in a format that will be especially valued as a classroom read-aloud." —*Bulletin of the Center for Children's Books*

An International Reading Association Teachers' Choice

DEAR AUSTIN:
LETTERS FROM THE UNDERGROUND RAILROAD

by Elvira Woodruff

The year is 1853, and eleven-year-old Levi Ives can't wait to join his brother, Austin, on the family claim out west. But for now, Levi is stuck back in Pennsylvania, writing to Austin and stirring up trouble with his friends Juniper and Possum.

Then tragedy strikes. Juniper's younger sister, Darcy, disappears, and all signs point to a horrifying explanation: slave catchers. Without telling a soul, Levi and Juniper set out on a perilous journey into the Deep South—not as master and slave, as some will assume, but as two terrified friends, desperate to find little Darcy before it's too late.

"Rich in adventure, mystery, and suspense."
—*School Library Journal*

"Woodruff combines swift pacing, historical detail, humor, depth, and precise characterizations for a wholly satisfying page turner."
—*Kirkus Reviews*